The Pantheon Hotel

A Ben & Bob Adventure

Bob Haider

Published by Bob Haider, 2024.

THE PANTHEON HOTEL

First edition. October 4, 2024.

ISBN: 979-8227200082

Written by Bob Haider.

Dedicated to Dr. Joshua Straus, Endeavor Health Medical
Group

My grateful acknowledgement is extended to my dear friend Ben Cusomato for his contributions to this piece.

Prologue

Bob took a break from his latest project and had several gulps of water. It was refreshing as he'd been laboring for several hours over a chemical formula he hoped to perfect which could be used in the battle against terrorists. As Bob paused in his latest endeavor, he gazed out the window of his apartment overlooking Rome's scenic Piazza Navona. 2,000 years before it was the site of an ancient circus where Romans watched brutal death games. Now the oblong oval is tranquil in comparison to that time and is now a popular tourist site. The center of the Piazza is dominated by a Bernini masterpiece—-the fountain of four rivers erected in 1651. It belies the fact anything violent could have happened here. Bob had visited Rome a couple of years ago and he was so fascinated with the city that he stayed.

Bob glanced at the clock on the wall and saw it was almost noon and time to eat. Bob enjoyed relaxing in the Piazza and lunching on pasta while enjoying a glass of fine Umbrian Chianti. In the evenings Bob enjoyed his dinners elsewhere in the many neighborhoods of Rome dining among the locals. One of his favorite dining spots was in the Trastevere neighborhood a short walk south.

Suddenly, the front door to Bob's apartment swung open with a resounding thud and in rushed Ben.

As Bob spun around at the sudden intrusion, he deadpanned, "What...not so much as a knock on the door or a ring of the bell?"

Before Ben could explain the urgency of his sudden arrival, he grabbed his handkerchief and swiftly brought it to his nose as he nearly gagged.

"My God, what is that horrific stench?"

"Oh, it's working then. It's hard to tell when you're around it all morning as I've been," Bob smiled widely.

"What is it?" Ben asked through his handkerchief.

"I'm devising a new formula. It is so foul it can be sprayed upon enemy terrorists while driving them to near madness and send them scurrying away."

"I can attest to that alright."

"It replicates human body sweat," Bob said proudly adding with additional specificity, "and it's a different kind of sweat than one would normally conjure when human sweat comes to mind as it's more along the lines of...,"

"My God man," Ben interrupted him, "why don't you save yourself a lot of time and just throw a bucket of crap at them?"

"Too manual," Bob answered perfunctorily.

"Well, what the hell...,"

"This could actually make them pass out if they don't evacuate the premises immediately. I envision it being used much like the gas in the movie *Goldfinger* when they did a fly over Fort Knox and the canisters were...,"

"Gas is right!" Ben shouted. "Come on. Let's get out of here. We've got more important matters to tend to. We're back on the job."

"Oh?"

"Yeah, why do you think I'm here?" he shouted rhetorically, as he headed toward the open door where he hoped the air would be more breathable.

As Ben stood in the hallway beyond the door while continuing to hold his handkerchief to his nose, he yelled, "I've got to pick up a few things for our next assignment so be out front and ready to go in thirty minutes."

"Anything in particular you want me to pack?"

"Bring the hologram device you perfected and the blueprint you devised on the DNA specific deterrent. I've got a plan and both of them will be of use to us," Ben instructed him, as he turned to leave, nearly gagged again, and added, "And for God's sake, open some windows on your way out or you'll be evicted by your landlord...if the residents don't kill you first."

Chapter 1

When Ben arrived precisely a half hour later and stepped out of a red fiat, Bob was waiting for him. As Ben approached, he noticed Bob wearing a headset and speaking into the mouthpiece. Ben waited for Bob's conversation to conclude, but when Bob saw Ben out of the corner of his eye, he immediately ceased talking.

"Tremendous! Are you ready to go?"

"I didn't want to interrupt while you were...,"

"What this?" Bob gestured to his headset, as he took it off. "Something I learned when I was on vacation once and needed to get my bearings. There was a fellow standing on the sidewalk who was on the phone so while I waited to ask for directions I perused my map. Well, he sees me and asks, 'Can I assist you in finding something?' I told him I didn't want to interrupt his call, and he says, 'Oh I only wear this for cover when I'm talking to myself. No one ever gives me a questionable look when I'm wearing my headset and naturally they don't know I'm having a conversation with myself,' he laughed. So, I started doing it and as you just saw...it works."

Ben's eyes rolled. He nodded as if feigning understanding. Nothing surprised him when it came to Bob's idiosyncrasies, as he pointed to Bob's arm.

"Are you alright? What happened? Why are you wearing a sling?"

"Oh, I heard a tip on the radio regarding floaters."

"What are floaters?"

"It's a condition I have...a deposit on the eye. Anyway, it's not serious and it's not constant; it comes and goes but it bugs the hell out of me because even though it's transparent it moves. It's like looking through a cobweb as a blur moves across the eye. Or sometimes it seems like your underwater and looking at something. It just blurs, you know?"

"Yeah, okay, but what's that got to do with the sling?"

"Though there's no cure for it, when I was listening to the radio, I heard a tip on how to make the condition a little better...a little less severe. It said to close your eye lids and then raise and lower your eyes gently behind your closed eyelids as if you were looking up and down. On those occasions when the blur returns for those of us who have floaters, it's an exercise that's supposed to make the condition a little better."

Ben nodded again feigning understanding but the look of confusion on his face betrayed him, which prompted Bob to add, "At the time I heard the tip on the radio, I was driving."

Ben shook his head. "You really need someone to watch over you," Ben commented facetiously.

"I thought that was your job," Bob smirked. "Aren't you like an older brother to me?"

"No amount of watching over you could help you from talking to yourself or keep you from driving with your eyes closed," Ben sniped.

"Good, then we understand each other. So, since you're here, it must mean it's time to go," Bob commented matter-of-factly.

"Do you have the DNA specific deterrent?"

"I do."

"Okay, let's go then," said Ben, as Bob walked around to the passenger's side of the car.

"Nice ride but a little snug," Bob commented, as he tossed his belongings into the back seat, got in and gave Ben some directions.

After they were on their way, Ben asked, "Was three months enough time for you to complete the preparations for this assignment?"

"Barely," Bob sighed. "I had to cajole them, beg them, promise them almost anything and that was just to get them to agree to attend. You wouldn't believe the logistical problems involved in getting 2,500 of them together for meetings reserving hotels, arranging meals for that many...,"

"Did you say 2,500?" Ben asked incredulously.

"Yep," Bob confirmed.

As Ben shook his head in disbelief, he commented, "I had no idea there were so many."

"Oh, yeah," Bob confirmed. "There are tens of thousands of them. I had to eliminate thousands just to get it down to 2,500."

Ben gazed toward his partner a moment and said, "Hmm, that could be a bit unwieldy." As Ben turned his gaze back to the road, he added, "Yeah that could definitely be a problem. I'll have to think about that as we drive."

"By the way, why are we driving from Rome to Venice? You usually call and have me meet you at the destination. I could have just met you there."

"I thought it would be nice for us to see the Italian countryside, maybe stop along the way get to know some of the Italian people."

"You do know I'm a bit of an introvert, don't you?" Bob stated.

"Oh, I know alright but that's exactly why I thought it would do you some good," Ben deadpanned.

"Meeting Italians is kind of tough to do if you're driving on thoroughfare at a hundred kilometers an hour," said Bob skeptically.

"I did say we might stop along the way."

"Well, I hope we stop somewhere because I haven't eaten. I was about to grab some lunch when you burst in."

Ben nodded his acknowledgement. "Don't worry, we'll stop for a bite."

As Ben drove through the city aided by Bob's directions, he observed the eternal city as they passed several of Rome's numerous exquisite fountains.

"Love the fountains," said Ben.

"There are over 2,000 in the city," said Bob.

As they took the bridge over the Tiber River, Ben saw the Castel Sant'Angelo on his right and soon they passed very close to the Vatican.

"We're heading a short distance west to pick up the highway going North to Florence and then we'll go in a Northeasterly direction to Venice.

"Okay, you're the guide," said Ben, and added, "Rome really is a nice city."

"It is indeed. I'm really glad I moved here. Without question, relocating to Rome was one of the best things I've ever done for myself."

"Yeah," Ben concurred.

"Hey," Bob interjected, as a thought occurred to him. "Could the fact we're driving from Rome have anything to do with you watching out for me and not wanting me to travel to Venice alone?"

"Yeah sure, that's it, little brother," Ben agreed.

"Hmm," Bob moaned unenthusiastically, as Ben pulled to a stop at a red light. "You'll continue going straight here."

They were on a four-lane road traversing Rome and Bob noticed that just beyond the intersection the road narrowed from four to two lanes rather quickly.

Bob glanced to his right as a sports car pulled up in the right lane.

The driver didn't turn right but waited along with them for the light to change.

Bob instinctively knew what the driver intended to do.

As nonchalantly as he could manage it, Bob turned toward Ben and asked,

"So, do you still carry that Glock with you wherever you go?"

"Yeah, it's in the glove compartment. Why do you ask?"

"Just curious," Bob shrugged, as he opened the glove compartment, grabbed the gun, flipped off the safety, leaned slightly out of their open convertible and as the traffic light turned green, he fired three shots into the driver's left front tire.

"No cuts, Pisano! Ciao!" Bob yelled.

Ben's calm demeanor was in part why he was so successful in the various endeavors in which the duo engaged. Ben was seldom rattled by anyone or anything. He believed being cool and composed was essential in his line of work. Though an adrenalin rush is nature's way of heightening one's senses by alerting one to danger, the adrenalin coursing through a person's veins can also rattle someone into making mistakes. In the midst of a dreadful and distressing situation, Ben possessed the capability of controlling his adrenalin rush and thus reduced the likelihood of human error.

Ben calmly glanced into the rear-view mirror to see if any law enforcement was in pursuit. Seeing no one, he turned his gaze and eyed Bob who was staring out the window.

"A little low on your medication there, Bob?"

"Ah, it's nothin'. He was gonna cut in. I just shot out his tire," Bob replied nonchalantly.

As Ben moved through the intersection, he glanced again into the rear-view mirror and saw the driver of the sports car put his hand in the air and make an obscene gesture screaming something but they were out of earshot.

Ben turned to Bob, and asked, "What was that he shouted?"

"I couldn't make it out exactly but I think he was attempting to swear in Italian," Bob replied.

"I thought you moved here because you liked Italy and Italians."

"What, that guy? He's a tourist. He's not Italian. He's driving a rental. He just shouted something in Italian because he thinks everybody that he bumps into in Italy is Italian.

"Oh, I see. I guess that's why his Italian is so bad," said Ben calmly, and added, "Well, I think you should put the gun away now. It's a long drive to Venice and we'll be passing...and be passed...by a lot of cars on the way."

"Hmm," was all that Bob muttered, as he slipped the Glock into his pocket rather than returning it to the glove compartment.

Ben drove the next fifty kilometers in absolute silence as the duo headed north. After forty-five minutes, the awkward silence between the two was palpable and it was Ben who initiated a conversation.

"You know...,"

Bob, who was staring aimlessly out the window, turned toward his partner in mild surprise.

"I...uh...never asked you how you persuaded everyone to attend our meetings in Venice. I mean, I know some of them can't stand being in the same room with each other. It must have been a very difficult task to say the least to convince them to attend."

"Egos," Bob answered nonchalantly as he continued to stare out the passenger's side window.

Ben immediately picked up on his partner's demeanor. He knew Bob quite well since their days in college and he was well aware of his tendency to retreat within himself...especially when he knew he'd been totally wrong in some action in which he engaged.

"What do you mean by egos?" Ben asked.

"Zeus, Jupiter, Poseidon, Neptune, Thor, Venus, Mars, Apollo you wouldn't believe what a high opinion all of them have of themselves."

Ben smiled, "Are you saying the gods have flaws? Isn't that an impossible dichotomy...for gods to have faults?"

Bob shrugged, "Perhaps but talk about conceit! Oh, man! After trying repeatedly to convince them to come to Venice, I finally realized all I had to do was to persuade one of them to attend. I simply said that so and so was going to participate in the conference and bam! Suddenly, they all want to attend. I'm telling you their egos are huge!"

"Hmm," Ben acknowledged with a smile, as he thought of the god complex.

"The real question is," Bob began, "despite the inflated opinion you have of yourself...,"

Hearing that, Ben knew Bob was out of his shell.

"How did a mere mortal like you contact the gods to begin with?" Bob asked. "I mean, they all knew you instructed me to contact them about attending the meetings. How did they know? How did you do that? How did you make that initial contact with the gods?"

After an appropriate theatrical pause, Ben responded with his patented sly smile, "You must have forgotten. I'm originally from Jersey. I have connections."

Chapter 2

While the duo drove north, a sudden burst of dust and dirt swirled into the air and obstructed their view.

"What the hell?" Bob yelled.

Remaining cool as ever, Ben slowed and steered the car to the shoulder and stopped.

"Good thinking partner," Bob commented.

"Maybe, if we don't get rear-ended."

Instinctively, Bob nervously turned to look out the back window but couldn't see a thing. Visibility was absolutely zero. Bob turned back toward Ben, and asked, "What do we do now?"

"We wait. Nothing else we can do."

Car horns blared both behind and in front of them as drivers hit their brakes and skidded against the roadway. Bob gulped, closed his eyes and prayed that a car didn't smash into them.

As gravity took hold, the dust and dirt slowly drifted downward covering the automobile in soot.

Ben hit the washer button and the wipers smudged the dirt. As Ben pumped the washer button several more times, the windshield began to clear and he peered into the distance with a steady stare.

Bob took a look toward the horizon but didn't know what object Ben's gaze focused upon.

When Ben began to nod, Bob asked, "What is it?"

"Hmm," Ben muttered, as he saw in the distance the cause of the sudden whirlwind.

"What do you see? What is it?" Bob repeated.

"Oh, we just need to take a little detour on our way to Venice," Ben stated matter-of-factly.

A confused expression crossed Bob's face which was not unusual for him. Ben often spoke in riddles until such time as he explained a situation more precisely. In their early assignments it annoyed Bob no end when Ben did that but over time Bob became more resigned to Ben's ways. Complaining to Ben about his lack of sharing details didn't do any good and it only served to get Bob more agitated. Bob would still mention it from time to time with a sarcastic remark or two but it didn't bother him as much nowadays...at least not nearly as much as it used to anger him. Besides, Bob knew there were things about his personality that annoyed Ben but as good friends do Bob accepted Ben's personality traits as Ben accepted Bob's sometimes erratic tendencies.

With visibility noticeably improved, Bob reclined his passenger's seat and settled back to doze until such time as Ben woke him to fill him in on the details.

Chapter 3

Ben slapped his open hand against Bob's shoulder, and beckoned him, "Time to wake up partner!"

A wide yawn opened and a long stretch ensued before Bob opened his eyes. When he rubbed his eyes and did finally open them, he saw they were parked on a rise.

"Come on," Ben urged him, as he exited the car.

Bob got out and followed as Ben directed him, "Stay low."

Bob did so and as they approached an overlook Ben got down fully into the prone position and Bob followed suit. They crawled to the edge of the overlook and peered at the scene below. Nestled in a shallow valley below was a small town that appeared peacefully tranquil with nothing out of the ordinary.

"I know this place," Bob commented.

"Oh," Ben commented. "Have you been here before? Have you ever traveled this way during your stay in Italy?"

"Well, I've been to Venice though I don't remember coming through here."

"We're off the main road," Ben stated.

Bob shook his head, "It looks familiar but I can't place it. Well, it'll come to me. So, why are we here?"

"We're here for the reason we're driving to Venice, said Ben, as he pointed toward a cave in the hillside across the valley. "They went in there."

"What did?"

"The creatures that kicked up all that dirt and dust," Ben explained, "the Creatures of Croatia."

"What? You mean the Creatures of Croatia are real? I thought they were a myth!"

"No myth, they're real all right."

"Well, are they like the story says?"

"Oh, yes. They are quite deadly. That's why we had to follow them."
Bob nodded in understanding.

"My contacts alerted me that the creatures flew across the Adriatic to Italy. That's about as far as they can fly without resting. They're so large they can't fly great distances without stopping to rest.

"Doesn't the myth make reference to the fact the creatures are hired out...like hired assassins?" Bob inquired.

"Like I said, they're not a myth," Ben replied, and added, "Somebody doesn't want us in Venice."

"What are we gonna do?"

From the moment his contacts informed him the Creatures of Croatia were on their way to Italy, Ben had thought through several scenarios and decided on what he intended to do.

Ben perused the horizon and saw they didn't have much time.

"Get your hologram device out," Ben instructed, which was one of Bob's greatest inventions. "The sun is setting and it'll be feeding time before we know it. We need to get to work; we've got a lot to do."

"What do you want me to create with it?"

"A ballpark...a full Major League Baseball Stadium...with aisles, seats, grandstands. I want everything. It must look fully authentic," Ben stated.

"Really?" Bob answered with delighted anticipation. "I always wanted to design my own ballpark."

"Well, now's your chance partner, but you'll have to do it quickly."

"That's not a problem. I could have it ready in less than thirty minutes. Is that quick enough?"

Ben grinned. "Yeah, that would be great. Centerfield must be there," Ben pointed into the distance. "I'm going to erect two light poles. I'll set them one hundred feet apart. Incorporate them into your stadium plan as two of the light towers since it'll be a night game."

"Any particular design you need it to be?"

"That's totally you're call partner. Just be sure the poles I place are beyond the centerfield fence and symmetrical with the hologram's light poles around the stadium so it's believable."

"So, there'll only be two actual poles," Bob clarified, "and the remainder I design in the hologram?"

"Correct," Ben replied.

Bob nodded his understanding, "Okay, got it."

"While you're creating that I'm going into the village to purchase flood lights, some tools and then I'll search for the appropriately sized metal poles that I can fit together and be the correct length for light towers."

"Okay, I'll get right on it. I should be finished by the time you get back."

"And if you finish before I return get going on the play by play."

"Huh?"

"You always wanted to be a baseball broadcaster. "You'll get your chance now."

"Oh, tremendous," Bob grinned, as he would soon fulfill a life-long dream.

"Bear in mind, you've got to get the attention of the populous and keep them listening. I don't care how you do it but get everyone to listen to your broadcast. There isn't any FCC here to stop you so you can say whatever you have to say in order to keep their attention. If the populous ventures out, the creatures will pounce. If you can keep the people distracted with your broadcast long enough, we might trap the creatures before they can do any harm."

"Leave it to me, Ben. I have plenty of ideas how I can keep the Italian countryside listening to their radios and watching their televisions."

Ben nodded his confidence and stated, "I know you will. I'll see you in a bit."

Suddenly, Bob shouted, "Udine Province!"

Ben turned abruptly, "What?"

"It came to me. This is Udine Province."

Ben wasn't at all sure how to respond to that as he didn't know anything significant about Udine Province and he reluctantly replied, "Okay."

Chapter 4

Bob put the finishing touches on the hologram design and hit the switch.

Instantly a major baseball stadium appeared complete with dugouts, meticulously manicured outfield and infield grass and an ivy-covered outfield wall comparable to Wrigley Field.

Bob designed the outfield dimensions as 330 feet down both the left and right field foul lines, 370 feet to the power alleys and 400 feet to straight away center field. The stadium was complete with box seats as well bleachers beyond the right and left field walls and an upper deck with grandstands in a semi-circle from the right field line around the backstop and stretching down the left field foul line.

With precise attention to detail Bob added the left and right field foul poles and the lighting on the top decks. He even added concession areas around the ball park and interspersed bathrooms for men and women to add to the realism.

Finally, his coup de gras was the addition of believable boisterous fans along with beer, wine and peanut vendors moving up and down the aisles. Bob was nearly ready to begin. He made the final adjustments to his broadcast apparatus that enabled him to break-in on all television and radio transmissions whether wireless, dish or land line. His broadcast would supersede all other communication for the surrounding area within a radius of one hundred miles. He even rigged social media so that all messages would be regarding his broadcast of this evening's 'game'. The populace would pay attention all right—-they'd have no choice. There was just one final thing Bob needed to tend to before he began.

From his bag Bob pulled out a device and placed it over his mouth. It looked very similar to an asthmatic's inhaler except that he placed it outside his mouth and straps which Bob tightened around the back of his head would hold the device in place.

It was another one of Bob's personal inventions...a translator. It activated on Bob's voice and his native English could be translated into any language merely be setting a dial. There was no more worrying about learning streams of vocabulary or concerns about using the proper tense. His patented device did it all.

Finally, Bob was ready to go as he took a deep breath and began his broadcast.

"Bonne soirée mesdames et messieurs."

Bob realized his mistake at once, loosened the straps and removed the translator.

"Missed it by a notch," he muttered as he reset the device from French to Italian and placed it back into position.

"Ciao!" he greeted his listeners speaking English into the translator which converted his words into perfect Italian.

Bob's invention of the automatic translator made the physical presence of a human translator obsolete. Additionally, he designed the device to recognize any grammatical errors he might verbalize in his native tongue. Those errors were automatically and literally 'lost in translation' as his device instantaneously corrected the errors.

He invented the translator many years ago and garnered a small fortune from the sales and the patent. Presidents and Heads of State never did use Bob's device as they preferred the human element rather than sit around a table with the unfashionable devices strapped over their mouths. But businessmen from countries all over the world took full advantage of it in their global dealings...at least for a time. Now they could opt to speak into their smart phones and a translation would be forthcoming in seconds.

"Welcome ladies and gentlemen," said Bob into the translator which redirected his words instantly into perfect Italian.

Many of the surrounding populace whether driving, or at home watching television or listening to Vivaldi on Venice Classic Radio immediately took notice as they thought their program had been interrupted to announce some catastrophic news event.

"We interrupt your normal programming for this special sports broadcast."

Within a hundred-mile radius thousands of Italian eyebrows creased upward into curious anticipation.

"Welcome to this evening's broadcast from Reno Bertoia Memorial Stadium in picturesque Udine Province where today the Udine Utes host the Milan Marauders."

In a village in Udine province in a home where four generations of one family resided, an elderly grandfather reacted in wide-eyed exuberance.

He arose quickly and shouted toward the bedroom, "Mama, mama, it's Reno! It's Reno!"

The grandfather's son came running nearly panic stricken at the sudden outburst.

"Papa what?"

"Call all of your cousins immediately, "Quickly, quickly! It's Reno," he repeated frantically, as he moved swiftly into the next room where his mother, great grandmother Bertoia, was resting. At 103 years of age, she hadn't heard him call out.

"Mama, mama, they're talking about Reno on the television!" he said, as he flicked on the small television in her room.

"They're talking about Reno on the radio too Papa," his son called to him.

Grandfather Bertoia exited the bedroom to see his grandchildren entering the living room and he waved his hands frantically as if gesturing them to get out of the house.

"Reno! Reno! It's Reno! Call your cousins now!" he repeated. Call everyone in town! It's Reno!"

Chapter 5

Ben was also listening on his phone while on his way back from completing his errands. He had rigged a harness around himself and dragged a sled behind him hauling two extremely heavy telephone-pole-sized wooden logs behind him.

"During this broadcast we'll feature interviews with some of the Udine Utes recorded earlier in the day. And that reminds me of a story when I first got started in broadcasting. I learned a lesson the hard way of why broadcasters interview ballplayers out on the field. Early in my career I was watching the ballplayers go through their paces and I didn't want to interrupt them while they did their running and stretching exercises as well as taking their turns in the cage for batting practice. I decided to wait and conduct the pre-game interviews in the locker room. Well, let me tell you, a confined clubhouse is not someplace you want to be an hour before game time after twenty-five athletes have exercised.

Ben chuckled heartily upon hearing that.

"So, enough said on that matter," Bob continued. "Our broadcast this evening is beamed throughout Europe and even into parts of Russia and the Mideast, so if our local listeners will bear with us for a few moments, I'd like to give our new listeners a bit of background and information."

Ben muttered under his breath, "He can't simply play it straight and broadcast a game," he shook his head, as he sweated and strained but steadily pulled his heavy load of materials. As Ben arrived, Bob looked up from his broadcast, pulled off his translator and said, "Hey, I'm making it up as I go along."

"No kidding," Ben chuckled, and added, "You know they've got smart phones that can translate now."

"Yeah, yeah, yeah," Bob muttered, as he put the translator back in place and returned to his broadcast.

"Reno Bertoia Memorial Stadium was named after Major League baseball player Reno Bertoia who was born right here in Udine Province January 8, 1935. In the 1940s American baseball fans followed the feats of Joe Dimaggio and rightly so. His exceptional play is best exemplified by his hitting in 56 straight games in 1941—-a feat that has yet to be seriously challenged. Well, with so many Italian immigrants in New York where Joe excelled for the Yankees, he acquired a hero's following in Italian neighborhoods. Joe was an Italian American unlike Reno Bertoia...a native of Italy.

"To place Reno Bertoia in historical context, he was actually one of the original bonus babies in America. He was signed under the bonus rule that was then in effect in American baseball in the 1950's, hence the nickname...bonus baby.

"What was the bonus rule, you ask? Well, I'll tell you. MLB put a rule in place in 1953 for anyone who signed a baseball contract for more than $4,000. Whoa! Yes indeed, I said a whopping $4,000. Big money back then. That was considered an enormous sum in 1953 to sign someone to a baseball contract who had never played in the Major Leagues up to that point.

"Now the bonus rule stipulated a player signed for that amount had to remain on the major league roster for two full seasons. That's right, they couldn't be sent to the minors to hone their skills and Reno Bertoia was among a number of players which included the likes of Al Kaline, Harmon Killebrew and Sandy Koufax.

"For those of you in our broadcast area that follow American baseball, it was because of that rule the great lefthander Sandy Koufax didn't do so well early in his career. Many figure filberts often cite statistics in the first years of his career as being less than exemplary. Well, he couldn't go to the minors to sharpen his skills, work on his control, perfect his curveball and harness his fastball with pinpoint control. Under the rule, Koufax had to stay with the Major League club.

"So now you know the story of Italy's very own, Reno Bertoia…a Major League baseball player remembered in his home province of Udine. So, let's get on with the game as we are ready for baseball."

"About time," Ben muttered, as he exhaled an exasperated sigh…not because of the hard work as he was in the process of digging two deep holes to hold the long poles in place. Bob's excessive talking had Ben shaking his head.

"Jack LoDuca is leading off for the visiting Milan Marauders. LoDuca, a switch hitter on the baseball field, is batting left-handed against the right-handed Mirko Petrovic who is on the hill today for the Udine Utes. Mirko is from Serbia and one could make a case that Serbian baseball players are to Italian baseball what Cuban players are to the United States. Petrovic was signed by the Utes after being pursued by many European ball clubs as well as many European States for his alleged involvement in war crimes but perhaps I shouldn't get into that.

"In Petrovic's last outing for the Utes, he lowered his overall season's E.R.A. to just under twelve when he allowed only five runs in four innings of work so we hope that trend continues this evening as he sets to throw the first pitch and get this game under way.

"And here's the pitch…,

"Whoa! LoDuca hits the dirt as Mirko Petrovic throws the first one at his ear hole. That was close! LoDuca gets up and brushes himself off. Boy, you can't beat fun at the old ballpark.

"Is that a peanut vendor in the background?" Bob asked rhetorically.

"Sounds to me like he has a bit of a lisp," said Bob, as he pulled the microphone away from his mouth, and threw his voice, "Penis! Hot penis! Penis here! Get your hot penis here."

Ben chuckled at that as he finished his excavation and wiped his brow.

"Well, I must say several ladies have jumped from their seats and are frantically waving in an effort to get that peanut vendor's attention, and I see a couple of gentlemen waving wildly as well."

Suddenly, but calmly, Ben overrode the system and interjected under his breath but loud enough so Bob could hear, "Can't you simply broadcast the game?"

"Well, my producer is whispering in my ear as LoDuca adjusts his batting helmet and steps back into the batter's box.

"Just as a modern baseball player adjusts his cup and jock strap, so too did ancient jurists of Rome adjust their thinking with the nuances of Roman law. Pax Romana in ancient Rome simply meant...ah...but I digress."

Ben, meanwhile, had gotten into the proper location where he strained and lifted one of the heavy poles into place and did so without even a pulley to assist him. He held the first pole upright while he kicked the dirt back into the hole packing the dirt with his feet and repeating the process all around the pole until he was satisfied it was secure.

"Mirko Petrovic toes the rubber and looks in for the sign from his catcher. I don't want to say that pitchers are mentally challenged, so let me just say there's a reason the catcher gives the signs and not the other way 'round and I'll leave it at that."

"Oh, God, please let him leave it at that and just broadcast a make-believe game," Ben muttered to himself.

"And here's the pitch. Oh, it's wide for ball two. Well, I must say the Utes have been on such a bad streak lately they recently lost both sides of an intra-squad game."

Ben rolled his eyes with that attempt at humor as he began working on the second pole.

"I asked the manager of the Utes, Victor Vitali, if he had time for an interview the other day. He said, 'Are you kidding? We can talk even during the game when I'm coaching third base because no one on this team ever reaches third. Coaching third base on this team I've got more free time than a professional golfer in Canada in December.'"

"Hmm," Ben muttered, as he nodded knowingly.

"On deck for the Milan Marauders is Wiley 'Doc' Miles. He was tagged with the nickname 'doc' because of the unauthorized animal experiments he conducted, but he was able to flee his country of Estonia before any charges were filed.

Ben was quite weary now from the strain of holding the next pole in place as he worked to fill in the second hole.

"Now this public service announcement," as Bob paused momentarily to feign the broadcast was breaking away from the game.

"For all you youngsters out there, when you're at the ballpark and need to use the facilities, be sure you wash your hands thoroughly with soap and water so you can prevent the spread of Germans."

Ben closed his eyes and shook his head, "All I asked him to do was broadcast a game," he muttered to himself, as he stomped on the dirt to compact it around the second pole.

Ben finished his task, as the two long poles flanked straight away centerfield beyond the hologram fence. They could have been light poles except that Ben had erected them without lights as he placed large batteries at the base of each of the poles. From the batteries he ran the electrical wires and rigged it all together while carefully covering the wires and batteries to avoid detection.

Ben interrupted Bob with a signal of his hand to cut the microphone.

Bob quickly concluded, "And in a close one the Udine Utes are edged by the Milan Marauders 15 to 0."

Ben explained, "The top of the pole is perfectly level and if my plan works each creature will be attracted by the light of the hologram. They will come out and if I'm correct they'll each sit atop one of the poles. When they do, you hit the switch for the electric current...zap! They're as dead as a bug in an electric insect trap.

Suddenly, Ben pointed. "Look, here they come!"

The grotesque creatures glided and circled the area but eventually they each alit on either of the poles exactly as Ben had predicted.

"Man, you did all that work to lug those poles all the way here, put everything together, dig the holes and then hold them upright while setting them into place. Damn! That must have been a Herculean task...utterly exhausting."

Ben nodded, satisfied with another task well done, as he said, "Yeah, but I've got to say it's worth all the effort and sweat when a plan comes together."

"Yeah, you came up with quite a plan to electrify them alright...or...you could have just," Bob said, as he reached into his pocket and pulled the Glock he'd used earlier, took dead aim at one of the creatures, fired and hit it between the eyes. Its head exploded into bloody pulp in a microsecond and before the other creature could react to the muzzle flash a projectile hit it between the eyes with the same result.

Ben, who was always cool and collected and never let things agitate him if events didn't go his way, became silently outraged...his lips pursed into livid infuriation while his eyes widened in angry ferocity.

Bob nonchalantly handed Ben back his handgun, and said, "I love you like a brother Ben but sometimes you really over think things."

Chapter 6

In just over five hours Ben and Bob were pulling into a car park as Ben steered into a parking spot and popped the trunk. Bob retrieved his two bags from the backseat and when Ben collected his they were ready to go.

"Wait! Wait! Wait!" said Bob, as he set the bags down and reached into his pocket.

"You're not gonna start shooting again, are you?"

"What?"

"You know, you might consider increasing the dosage of your medication," Ben suggested.

"What? No, no, no," Bob chortled. "This is something I've been working on that you...,"

"Not another crappy formula!" Ben protested.

"No! No! I've been working on a universal remote ignition. I can start any car. You've got to see this! It will work on absolutely any car regardless of who manufactured it. See that yellow sports car about the middle row in?" Bob asked.

"Yeah," Ben replied.

"Watch," said Bob, as he aimed the remote toward the center of the car park.

Instantly, the trunks of every automobile in the car park opened simultaneously.

Ben's eyebrows arose. "It looks like your latest endeavor needs a little fine tuning. Come on, Einstein," he said, as they exited the car park.

"I don't understand it," Bob muttered, as he stared at his latest device. "It worked before."

"Shake it off, partner," said Ben chuckling.

Bob changed the subject, and asked, "You think our rental will be safe in the car park?"

"Sure, it's patrolled," Ben lied to alleviate Bob's concern. "Besides if any thieves appear I'm sure they'll be content simply to rob the cars whose trunks are already open," he said, as they walked to the dock to purchase their tickets, took a seat and waited for the next water taxi to arrive.

On a near-cloudless day the Adriatic Sea glistened and twinkled as the warm Mediterranean sun bounced off the tranquil waters. Bob took a deep breath pulling in as much of the rich sea air as he could, exhaled and said wistfully, "God, I already love it...here by the sea."

While they were waiting Bob changed gears and began to complain about their current assignment.

"You wouldn't believe how much planning has gone into this and I'm not just saying that to brag about my effort. These guys...uh...gods, well...it was really difficult to get them all together in one place. Egos aside, they're unbelievably busy."

"Hmm," Ben sighed.

"But we've got great representation. "I believe there are a dozen Slavic gods confirmed, sixteen Mesopotamian, seventeen Egyptian, twenty-three Chinese, forty-eight Roman, fifty Greek gods...,"

"Wait a minute," said Ben, as something Bob said suddenly clicked in.

"Did you say Mesopotamian gods?"

"Yeah, there are sixteen of them, why?" Bob questioned.

Mesopotamia doesn't even exist anymore."

"Well, it's Iraq now, but that's the way it works—-once a god, always a god."

"Couldn't you have done something like baseball does?"

"What do you mean?"

"Well, couldn't you have divided them up into some kind of a Major and Minor League kind of thing? And then just invited the Major gods?"

"Oh, let me tell you, if I dared categorize just one of them as a minor god...with the egos they have...well there'd be no end to their wrath. They'd have had me skewered alive. I'm telling you. These guys are brutal."

Ben rubbed his face, as he contemplated the situation silently mulling over several ideas in his mind.

After a while, he said, "The sheer number of attendees is going to complicate the mission but we'll work around it. I might be able to do something about that."

"Hmm," Bob nodded.

"I suppose they're going to be spread all over Venice since there isn't a hotel large enough to accommodate all of them."

"Oh, you won't believe this. There's a new hotel. Several investors bought a string of mansions on the Grand Canal, connected them, renovated, even raised the ground floor, and considering who is going to stay there you'll never guess what they named their new hotel?" he asked rhetorically, and continued, "The Pantheon Hotel."

"Hmm," Ben muttered.

"Yeah, how's that for a coincidence? And it's supposed to be spacious and gorgeous."

"What do you mean, 'supposed to be'? You haven't seen it?" Ben asked incredulously.

"Well, I saw brochures...looked at it online."

"Well, what about conference rooms, do they have enough space to accommodate 2,500?" Ben inquired.

"Oh, well," Bob stammered, "they're big conference rooms. I'm sure they'll accommodate a goodly number of...,"

"Well, I guess that means no," Ben gazed out over his brow in displeasure and continued. "We'll have to conduct our meetings publicly...in Piazza San Marco perhaps."

"That would certainly be a large enough venue as long as it doesn't rain," said Bob.

"I'll think of something to winnow down the number," said Ben.

"They're going to be awfully pissed if you tell some of them to leave."

"Yeah, I'll have to do it in a way that makes it their idea while ensuring others wish to remain."

"Good luck with that."

"Do you have any dinners planned?"

"Oh, yeah, just like Corporate America does," Bob replied confidently. "I've got dinners planned for each evening after the meetings."

"Oh?" Ben questioned.

"Well, the dinners might be a problem because the restaurants in Venice are all tiny. It's tough to seat one hundred...let alone locating one that will seat twenty-five hundred in one sitting."

Ben eyed Bob with a look of severe derision. "Yes, about twenty-five times more difficult no doubt," Ben noted.

"Oh, but listen, for entertainment as the conference is concluding, I've planned a golf outing, you know, because we need to plan some relaxation time. It'll be just like corporations do when they have those bogus off-site meetings at resorts. I contacted both of our old college roommates."

"Oh?" Ben questioned.

"Yeah, Jack manufactures and sells golf carts and golf cars, though I'm unclear on what the difference is between the two. Anyway, I've talked to him about shipping twelve hundred and fifty carts...that's one for every two golfers, as there are two to a cart. I even contacted Don who's still doing his meteorological work in Oklahoma City. He told me that the weather forecast for Venice is supposed to be perfect for the day I'm planning the outing. Talk about paying attention to details," said Bob proudly.

"Well, let's see," Ben rubbed his chin, then reached into his pocket and pulled out a small calculator, while Bob looked in to see what his partner was doing.

"I hate to burst your bubble but lets' see if there are any details you may have overlooked."

"Okay," Bob said uneasily as he shifted in his seat.

"First, let's do the math. Let's figure the first tee off will be six o'clock in the morning."

"That sounds right," Bob agreed.

"And let's push it and figure a foursome teeing off every 7 minutes. That's almost nine foursomes every hour, but what the hell let's round up to ten foursomes per hour just for the sake of figuring this out. That's ten times four which is forty gods teeing off every hour."

"Yeah, okay," Bob nodded enthusiastically in agreement.

"Now let's divide forty per hour into 2,500."

Bob nodded silently and uneasily.

"Well, what do you know?" Ben asked mockingly. "All we'll need is just over 62 hours for each of them to get in one round of golf!" Ben yelled. "62 hours! And oh yeah—-Venice is full of canals! There are no golf courses in Venice!" Ben screamed."

"What?" Bob asked astounded.

"How's that for attention to details?" Ben questioned.

Bob's shoulders slumped immediately in disappointment as the realization hit him hard. "Dammit!" he muttered under his breath.

Almost immediately Ben felt badly for yelling. "Ah, hell, don't worry about it. Maybe there's a golf course on the mainland that's not too far," said Ben, trying to ease Bob's tattered self-esteem, as Ben's cell phone sounded.

Bob watched as Ben answered and listened intently. Bob observed the irritation moving across Ben's face as if something had gone wrong.

"No, not Vegas, we're meeting in Venice!" Ben clarified. "Yes, Fortuna, I realize you're the goddess of good fortune but you don't have to physically be in Vegas to bring good luck to those who are there," he said, shaking his head. "Look, we'll be keeping transcripts of everything that's discussed, just get here as soon as you can and we'll get you caught up." Ben disconnected, as he shook his head in exasperation, and turned to Bob. "That was...,"

"Yeah, I got the gist," Bob chuckled, as a breeze off the Adriatic brushed cool against their faces. "Well, at least I'm not the only one that messed up;" Bob shrugged, and with an ever-widening smile he added, "Who knew gods make mistakes?"

Chapter 7

The water taxi arrived and as they boarded, Ben said, "You understand that once the god's enter earth's atmosphere, they take on physical form, right?"

"Yeah, ala Christ," Bob nodded. "How'd you get them all to agree to that?"

"New Jersey persuasion," Ben chuckled, "I told them...,"

Bob abruptly raised a hand. "Wait! On second thought, I don't want to know how you persuaded them."

Ben shrugged, "Okay."

"But aren't you the least bit concerned that they could have dire consequences to your physical well-being? I mean, they can get just as tough or tougher with you."

"Well, that would be revenge and gods aren't allowed to partake in that," Ben laughed.

"I think they do take revenge," Bob muttered, "they simply call it wrath."

"Anyway, if we're going to sit down together, to talk and work things out, we've got to be able to see each other and hear one another or it isn't going to work. Besides, it's more about physics than it is about them agreeing to take on physical form. They created the world in which we live and they have to abide by the rules they put in place. When they thirst, they'll drink; when they hunger, they'll eat; and when they get mad, they'll lose their temper and perhaps use a few choice words they wouldn't normally use in polite conversation."

"Okay, I get it. It's a world of physics...except for miracles," Bob pointed out.

"Yeah, and you let me know when you see one of those miracles," Ben replied snidely.

When the water taxi changed its heading from easterly to north around the tiny island of San Giorgio Maggiore, Bob's eyes alit with joy. Piazza San Marco came into view punctuated by the 325-foot-tall Campanile, an Italian word meaning bell tower, that loomed ahead dominating the Square.

Along the water's edge sleek shiny gondolas bobbed gracefully at their moorings as if beckoning new visitors to board them and glide through the magnificent canals of Venice.

The splendid Grand Canal, which headed past majestic palaces on the water's edge, touched Bob in a way in which nothing before ever had. Bob viewed the picturesque scene spread out before him in wide-eyed awe as he was seeing Venice for the first time in his life. On the right he saw the Palazzo Ducale, or Doges Palace, where for hundreds of years the Doges resided as the rulers of Venice.

Situated between the bell tower and the regal palace a single column arose topped by a horizontal platform supporting the dignified winged-lion, symbol of Venice's power and prestige, as if it were a watchful immovable guard standing pillar-like in stately vigilance over the city.

"I think this is the most exquisite site I have ever seen in my life. If there is a more gloriously beautiful approach to any city on earth, I haven't seen it," Bob commented, as he began shaking his head in disappointment.

"What's the matter?" Ben asked.

"I just can't believe I'm about to visit Venice with you," he glanced toward Ben.

"You live in Italy and you hadn't visited Venice before this?"

"No, I was saving it to go with my girlfriend."

"Oh, well, you never mentioned you have a girlfriend."

"Presently, I don't. That's why I was saving this trip…for when I do meet a special lady."

"Oh," Ben acknowledged. "Well, you're not exactly my first choice either, but now that we're in Venice stop whining."

"I'm not whining," Bob protested.

As the water taxi was now within a hundred yards of the dock, Ben turned and observed his partner's gyrations with a perceptive but confused eye.

Bob reached inside his jacket and pulled out an odd shaped instrument with several gauges and scanned the shoreline with a discerning eye. Bob nodded in confirmation of his findings as if he expected his instruments to register a reading.

"Something foul is afoot in Venice," Bob declared with great certitude.

Ben smirked, "The sea water may be a bit stagnant near the shore; perhaps that's the scent you've detected," he ventured.

Suddenly, the duo witnessed a man standing up in a gondola to take a picture of Piazza San Marco and the Doges Palace. The man teetered one way, then the other, lost his balance and fell from the gondola. He flailed in the water desperately as he attempted to swim toward shore.

Bob pulled out his stopwatch, and commented nonchalantly, "Speaking of miracles, here we go again," as he clicked the stopwatch as Ben immediately jumped in and swam briskly toward the man in trouble.

Bob removed another small instrument from one of his pockets and held it in his other hand measuring the exact distance between the water taxi and the man in the water.

Ben swam so rapidly he'd be the envy of a dolphin.

Bob clicked the stopwatch just as Ben clasped the man in a lifeguard's grip, while Bob looked through the viewer of his instrument and calculated the exact distance.

As Ben swam toward the water taxi with the man in tow, Bob shouted out to him. "The distance was exactly fifty meters," as Bob glanced at his stopwatch, "which means you took a full second off your previous time, so you're down to seventeen seconds flat."

Bob then cupped his hands together and hollered, "That's nearly three seconds faster than the Olympic 50-meter record," Bob smiled widely adding, "and that's with your clothes on," Bob shook his head, always astounded at Ben's displays of physical prowess.

Suddenly, Bob saw something in the water behind Ben closing fast. Bob saw a serpent-like head with a long snout...its mouth agape exposing sharp teeth that glistened in the sunlight. The dragon-like body both bowed above the water line and submerged beneath it as it moved through the water closing quickly on its would-be prey...Ben and the man he rescued.

"Swim like hell, Ben!" Bob screamed, "A creature is closing in on you! Hurry!"

With the deftness of an Olympic swimmer who is also highly trained in the art of gymnastics, Ben spun around and from beneath the water kicked his leg and caught the creature just below the snout. The force of Ben's perfectly timed kick catapulted the creature fully ten meters into the air before it fell splashing limply into the lagoon disappearing below the surface.

The onlookers on the water taxi were awed by Ben's athletic display while several passengers leaned over the side to assist Bob in helping Ben get the man safely aboard.

As they did so, Bob stepped back and nodded as if acknowledging the rescued man and recognizing him immediately. The man sported a full beard, strong muscular arms and had continued to cling to a three-pronged pitch fork the entire time that Ben and the others were getting him out of the water. He looked exactly like the pictures depicting Neptune as he came out of the sea but he was no taller than 5' 9" or 5' 10" tops.

"Are you all right, Neptune?" Ben asked.

Neptune coughed up salt water, and nodded, "I think so. Thanks for pulling me out. I don't swim as well as I used to."

"That's all right. Glad I was there to help," Ben patted him on the shoulder, "but Neptune, I've told you before, you're not the god of the seas," Ben chided him, pointing out, "That's an old myth. You're the god of irrigation but the canals in Venice are liquid highways. They're not for irrigation and they're unforgiving."

Neptune coughed up some more salt water and nodded that Ben was correct.

"Nevertheless, it is good you are here for the conference."

Ben turned and noticed Bob's surprise. "I told you, physics. They've all got to fit through the doors, into their hotel rooms, ride in gondolas, so they're human size," Ben clarified. "And don't let that creature throw you. I have a feeling we're going to be seeing a lot of strange things in Venice during our assignment."

Bob paused for a moment, still distracted by Ben's amazing feat, and asked, "Where was it again that you learned to swim like that?"

"Learned to swim like that?" Ben chuckled. "Learning had nothing to do with it; it's a gift," Ben smirked, "but I honed my natural born skills during one summer on the Jersey shore of course."

Chapter 8

Ben was correct. An assembly of 2,500 gods in Venice is only possible at Piazza San Marco. As they were gathering in the square, Ben and Bob were busily checking off the names of those in attendance, while Ben commented, "I still can't believe you invited all of them."

"Hey, next time you want to get the gods assembled, you try doing it."

"All right, all right, calm down," Ben tried to soothe his feelings.

"Oh, yeah, you criticize me and then you tell me to calm down."

"Down and out," Ben blurted out.

It was his habit whenever Bob got overly agitated Ben would mention something that went back to their days of intramural football at Oklahoma. Ben was the most talented quarterback in the league, while Bob was a gifted receiver with great speed. They had teamed up on many a touchdown tosses, so to occasionally calm Bob, Ben simply barked out a pass pattern.

Bob nearly glowed with joy as he reminisced in his mind. "Oh, those were good days, weren't they?"

"Works every time," Ben whispered under his breath.

As Ben returned his attention to the list of attendees, Bob pointed out the magnificence of the façade of St. Mark's.

"As legend has it," Bob began, "Venetian merchants stole the bones of the Evangelist, St. Mark and this beautiful basilica which dates back to 1063 is home to his relics. The building is a gothic masterpiece that has largely remained in its present form, though the outside of the basilica has changed substantially over the centuries. Of note are the four bronze horses above the main entrance. The originals were taken in 1204 during the Fourth Crusade from Constantinople although some historians believe they date to the time of the Romans. In any event, nearly eight hundred years later they were stolen by Napoleon only to have them taken back in 1815. The originals were placed inside the basilica's museum and those on the outside are copies."

Suddenly there was a commotion as the crowd gasped in awe at what they saw, as many of the gods pointed toward the top of the basilica. Ben turned around to see the bronze horses had grown wings and gracefully floated downward toward the square. Ben spun around quickly, stared at the gods, the look of displeasure evident on his face, as he began to slowly scan the crowd with a keen eye.

When Ben spotted Epona, his nostrils flared in anger at the horse goddess.

"Epona, this is not a joke and we have very serious business to conduct during our Venetian conference, so if you don't mind, I'd appreciate it if you would dispense with the Pegasus humor. The famous bronze horses of Venice do not sport wings," said Ben sternly.

Epona nodded reluctantly and with a flick of her hand, the wings disappeared and the bronze horses crashed to the pavement below shattering to pieces.

"That's it!" Ben shouted. "You're dismissed!"

Bob viewing all of this leaned in, and whispered, "Post pattern over the middle," and chuckled within himself.

"It doesn't work in reverse," Ben snapped angrily.

"You can't dismiss me, I'm a god!" Epona protested vehemently.

"I am in charge here," Ben retorted curtly, "and you are dismissed," he pointed toward a walkway that exited from the Square.

Epona's eyes flashed in anger as she approached Ben.

The gods in attendance wondered what she was going to do as she neared their host.

She leaned in toward Ben and whispered so that no one else could hear her, "Remember, you owe me for this."

Playing his part, Ben straightened up, and shouted, "Out!"

Epona playing her part magnificently appeared to be quite reluctant but nevertheless departed seething in anger.

Ben then turned toward the gods, and announced adamantly, "Make no mistake. I am in charge of this meeting. Test me and you will be gone in a heartbeat."

One of the gods raised his hand while he coughed up some additional sea water from the lagoon.

Ben pointed toward him, "Yes, Neptune, you have a question?"

Bob looked up from his clipboard, as Neptune said, "Ah, some of us were wondering if we...uh...I mean since there are so many of us."

"Yes, yes, what it is it? Speak up," Ben prodded him.

"We're wondering if we all have to attend...that is...if Epona gets to leave...,"

"Am I to understand that some of you wish to leave?" Ben asked in mock surprise, as the conniving wheels spun ever so quickly in Ben's ever-scheming mind.

Ben's ploy was totally unbeknownst to Bob, as he leaned in toward his partner and Bob said, "Wait a minute. I just had a thought of how to winnow down this massive group and this may be the break we need."

"It's okay," Ben replied. "Let me take this," he said, as he looked out over the throng in attendance, and said, "Please go on, Neptune," Ben prompted him.

"It's just that there are so many of us...do you really need all of us to attend the conference?"

"Well, I don't think it would be quite fair to the group simply to dismiss some of you."

"We could draw lots," yelled one of the gods.

"Have a lottery," yelled another.

"Draw straws," shouted another.

Ben raised his palms to quiet and settle the gods. "Let me consult on this. Just a moment," he said, as he turned toward Bob.

"I think I've got them where I want them now. Just nod a couple of times as if you're agreeing with me in some discussion. Now you pretend to talk, just mouth some words, and I'll nod my head."

After a few moments of this back-and-forth fictional discussion, Ben turned toward the crowd of gods, and said, "Give us a few minutes and we'll have a drawing that I think will be fair to everyone."

2,500 gods emitted an enthusiastic yelp that echoed throughout Piazza San Marco.

Chapter 9

"They dare to ignore me!" shouted an enigmatic figure, as his voice echoed in a musty, abandoned mansion in Venice. "I am the greatest of all the gods! How dare they slight me!" the entity snarled indignantly.

Though his face was obscured in the dark of the unlit room, the entity's evil snarl could be seen from the minute amount of sunlight that streamed into the room between the shadows. Plaster had peeled from the walls of the neglected mansion and lay haphazardly upon the floor that had not been swept for years.

The entity was seated at a table with no tablecloth. Several places were set for a lunch that had already been served and eaten, the dirty dishes not yet cleared, while rats scurried about the room in search of morsels for their survival that might have fallen from the table.

Suddenly, the entity slammed his fist angrily upon the table. The silverware and dishes bounced upward, clanked and rattled loudly while dust from the table arose in thousands of tiny specs of a cloudy haze.

Two of his underlings were seated at the table. One bowed his head to ensure he would not make eye contact as he did not wish to be within his crosshairs and suffer the full extent of his boss's wrath. Indeed, on various occasions in the past, the entity had a number of his minions put to death for nothing more than disagreeing with him. To disagree with this entity when he was not in the mood for opposition, always risked death.

The other subordinate at the table was the more confident of the two. He ventured to speak but judiciously chose his words carefully. "Perhaps, if I may suggest, what is perceived as a slight was nothing more than a simple oversight."

"Silence!" the entity admonished him vehemently. He wallowed in his contempt and would not be denied his moment of anger. Only his interpretation of events would be tolerated.

"I am not a bourgeois interpreter of inane human intentions! I was the greatest god of my time! Once a great god, always a great god! How dare they forget me!" he vented, as he paused to consider what he was going to do next.

The underling leaned toward his boss, as if he were about to advise him on a matter of great import as advisors often do. He lowered his voice to a hushed tone as if speaking in confidence, as he commented, "All the gods are gathering in Venice."

"Tell me something of which I am not already aware," he snapped at his subordinate in facetious contempt.

"You defeat them here...this duo Ben and Bob. You defeat them by yourself without the aid of the others gathered in Venice and you will surely be declared the greatest god of all by all of those in attendance," he suggested, as a self-assured smile flashed across his face.

The entity contemplated his subordinate's suggestion, envisioned the glory and the resulting free reign he would enjoy throughout the nations of the world. He rubbed a reflective index finger back and forth across his upper lip. Yes, it was all there for the taking, he concluded. After considering the matter with an opportunistic air as well as with an optimistic outcome, his naturally skeptical mind turned toward his underling, and he asked, "What is in it for you?"

A smirk flashed across the minion's face, as he admitted, "Money, wealth."

"Hmm, yes of course, exactly what all of you who serve me seek," the entity stated confidently but with derision.

The self-confident minion gestured in a slight nod and dip of his head, acknowledging the correctness of his master's perception.

"That duo has been a thorn in my side long enough!" the entity bellowed, as he gestured for one of the servants standing against the wall, a briefcase in hand, to approach him. The servant did so and handed the briefcase to his master and without turning his back, backpedaled until he was once again in position against the wall.

The entity opened the briefcase, retrieved a thick wad of euros and with his long, bony fingers pushed the stack across the table tracing a path in the dust toward his underling, and said, "Succeed, and there will be more to follow."

"The thought of failure never enters my thinking," the subordinate replied with a satisfying smile.

"No one in my employ plans on failure," the entity smirked. "Nevertheless, bones are strewn across Europe of those who have botched their assignments," he remarked flatly, leaving no doubt what would happen to the self-assured minion if he did not succeed.

"Now you'd better prepare quickly," the entity continued. "There is no time to lose. Use your eyes and ears. Learn why they have come to Venice and report back to me. Take no action and tell no one but me."

"I understand completely," the subordinate acknowledged his master's instructions.

The underling arose from his chair, glanced at his intimidated colleague who had been too afraid to speak and flashed a contemptuous smirk in his direction. He turned back toward his master who gestured with a flick of his wrist for him to approach.

Thinking he would receive some additional instruction on his assignment, he inquired, "Yes, sire?"

The entity nodded in the direction of the man's colleague, and said, "I shall have him eliminated as I have no need in my service for such a timid, fearful insect of a human being."

Chapter 10

It was just a matter of minutes and Ben was ready to go with several scraps of paper inside a hat, though unbeknownst to the gods the drawing would be anything but random or fair.

Ben raised his hand, paused, and called out to the crowd, "Is everybody ready?"

2,500 gods responded in resounding cheers, as Ben reached into the hat and pulled out the first scrap of paper. Though each piece of paper had only an unreadable scrawl, Ben announced, "The first group of you that does not have to attend the conference is any god that...," Ben paused for effect as he eyed the multitude, and continued, "has anything to do with fertility, love, or any form of forni...,"

A roar of applause thundered through Piazza San Marco before Ben could finish his sentence as fully more than half the gods arose and threw their hats in the air reminiscent of graduation at the U.S. Naval Academy in Annapolis, Maryland.

Bob, his mouth agape, turned toward Ben, and said, "I didn't realize there were so many gods that had something to do with...,"

"Yeah," said Ben in acknowledgement aware of what Bob was about to say.

"They're really excited to skip the conference," Bob chuckled.

"Well, their excitement is understandable," Ben smirked. "The gods of love have been loosed in Venice of all cities," he said, as Ben's smirk moved into a wide smile. "At one time there were nearly 12,000 registered, taxpaying ladies of the night in Venice. They'd sit in their windows and flash their wares to passing potential customers. Of course, I don't know how many there are now, but oh the gods...they are going to have a good time this weekend."

"Hmm," Bob muttered.

Many of the gods scrambled and elbowed their way past their fellow gods in an effort to exit the Piazza. On their way out, several of the gods passed Ben and Bob including Aphrodite and Venus. Ben nodded them adieu as he said, "So, do you ladies have a favorite outfit for your first evening in Venice?"

"I don't know about Venus," Aphrodite cooed, "but I'm going to wear my slinkiest, most stylish ensemble!" she said with an air of confidence, as she sashayed away.

One of the gods raised a questioning hand and Ben acknowledged her, "Yes, Hera?"

Hera arose, and asked, "Juno and I, as protectors of marriage, were wondering if we could also...that is...if we qualify for skipping...,"

Ben smiled widely. "Yes, indeed, Hera, you and your counterpart Juno may leave if you wish."

Both of the gods nodded happily and departed.

Ben raised the hat again and picked another slip of paper from it.

"Next, those who need not attend the conference are any gods regarding wind, rain, lightning, hail, storms of any kind, and...what the heck...all weather."

Aeolus, the king of the winds led the gods of the north wind, west wind, south wind, and east wind out of the Piazza while hundreds more arose and left, as another one of the gods still in attendance raised his hand.

"Yes, Pusan," Ben recognized him.

The Hindu sun god arose, and asked, "You know, the sun sending its warmth to earth has a great deal to do with the weather here, so cannot the sun gods...,"

Ben quickly adlibbed, "Why, yes indeed it does! In fact, not only the sun gods, but also those of the moon, the stars and all the planets," he chortled, "as the tug of the planets and the gravity have an effect on the earth's weather."

Yet again hundreds more whooped in ecstatic delight as they departed the Piazza.

"We are now ready for the third and final draw," Ben announced, as another uproarious cheer echoed throughout the square.

Ben raised his hand and plucked the next bogus scrap of paper from the hat.

An anxious lull hung over the remainder of the gods gathered in San Marco as Ben examined the piece of parchment delaying purposely so as to add to the drama.

He raised his gaze and announced, "The final exemption for the conference is hereby awarded to...," Ben hesitated, and with a sly smile glanced at Bob, and continued, "trees, flowers, barley, oats, grains and vegetation of any kind."

A roar of delight erupted, enveloped and shook the square as hundreds more gods sped away to enjoy their weekend in Venice.

Saturn as the protector of Sowers and seeds raised his hand. "Technically, it's not vegetation as yet because it hasn't germinated but...,"

"Yes, Saturn, you may leave as well," Ben smiled, "in addition to Pomona and Vertumnus as the protectors of orchards and gardens.

Bob looked out over the remaining gods...a mere smidgeon that remained from the original twenty-five hundred. "If those of you who remain will please follow us, we'll head over to the Pantheon Hotel to get you registered and checked-in.

Ben gestured to Bob as they were departing, and said, "I really think it was foolish to name a new lodging in Venice...The Pantheon Hotel. A lot of people are going to be confused thinking they're making reservations in Rome."

"Oh, no. There are lots of cities with Pantheons. Paris has a Pantheon; London has a Pantheon; Madrid, the Pantheon of Illustrious Men; Lisbon, the National Pantheon and many other cities as well."

"My point is when you say, 'The Pantheon', there's one place specifically that comes to mind."

Bob shrugged, "Well, maybe," as he directed the gods, "This way, please."

Chapter 11

Ben and Bob stood in the lobby of the Pantheon Hotel, clipboards in hand checking off names, as the gods entered.

Suddenly, an obviously frantic concierge raced up to them in a very frenetic manner, and before he could say anything, Bob acknowledged him, and asked, "Yes? What is it?"

The concierge motioned to a distant point in the hotel, and stammered, "There's a man...uh...,"

Ben turned to Bob. "I'll take care of this. You handle the check-in," he said, as he followed the concierge.

Meanwhile a bearded man with brown hair, soft features and dressed in a flowing white robe approached the front desk.

"Yes, sir, may I help you?" asked the clerk.

"I'm here for the conference. I have a reservation."

"And you are?"

"I am, who Am," he shrugged.

"Yes, well, that's very nice," the clerk replied tongue in cheek, as he thought...*What the hell is that supposed to mean?*

"I'll need a name sir, it's how we track our reservations, you see."

"Ah," he nodded in understanding. "Jesus."

The clerk's eyebrows upturned, as he clarified, "Just the one name?"

"Hmm," Jesus nodded.

The clerk typed quickly on his keyboard and shook his head. "I'm sorry, nothing's coming up."

"Hmm, you know, Jesus is Aramaic for Joshua. Try Joshua."

The desk clerk typed in the name, and shook his head, "No. Nothing under Joshua."

"Oh, oh," Jesus replied in excitement. "Try Jesus of Nazareth."

The clerk nodded, and repeated, "Jesus Nazareth," but again shook his head. "Sorry, still no good."

"Christ...,"

"Excuse me, sir?" the clerk took offense, as he was taken aback.

"Try Christ," he clarified. "It seems many people mistakenly think Christ is my last name, so maybe the reservation is listed under that. Try Jesus Christ."

The clerk again typed speedily but alas once again shook his head. "I'm very sorry, sir, but nothing at all is coming up under any of those names."

"Son of a bitch," Jesus yelled, "I don't believe this is happening again! Once as a child and now as an adult!"

A man in a silver mask leaned in from behind him, and said, "The fact there was no room at the inn, well, technically that happened to your parents."

"Well, I was there too!" Jesus snapped.

"Not really," the masked man shook his head, "you hadn't been born yet."

"I am infinity! Erstwhile, I was there!" Jesus yelled, as he realized finally who it was behind him. "Mohammad?"

The masked man nodded.

"I should have known. The mask," said Jesus. "It's the no images thing, right?"

"You got it. It's not just me though."

"No," Jesus agreed. "It's the Jewish god, the Islamic god, and you, Mohammad—-no images."

"Yeah, that's right," Mohammad nodded.

"Ah," Jesus bemoaned, "when are you ever gonna get over yourself?"

"Excuse me?" Mohammad demanded.

"Don't give me that holier than thou attitude," Jesus retorted, as a thought suddenly struck him, and he added, "Hey, come to think of it. Why are you here? This conference is for the gods. You're not a god. You're just a prophet."

"Hey, in my faith YOU are only a prophet!" Mohammad challenged him.

"You, Mohammad, are a bit too pompous for your own good," Jesus admonished him.

"You go too far, Jesus! No man talks to me in that manner," as Mohammad placed his hand on his scabbard ready to reach for his sword.

"Yeah?" Jesus shot back at him challenging his potential threat.

Mohammad snarled, "For the first three centuries after your death a schism developed among your adherents between those who thought you were a man and those who believed you were a god."

"Not A god...THE Son of God," Jesus corrected him.

"To breach that schism in the Christian faith it was mere mortals who proclaimed your divinity at the first Council of Nicea. That is where the doctrine of your divinity was formally affirmed and that was three hundred years after you died," Mohammad rebuked him.

"Uh, excuse me," the clerk intervened.

Simultaneously, their heads turned abruptly toward the clerk and they shouted in unison, "Mind your own business!"

Jesus turned back toward Mohammad and noted, "In any event, I didn't simply die; I was executed. I was crucified by the Romans," Jesus noted, and with an outstretched index finger pointed at Mohammad's chest added emphatically, "and I arose again...on the third day. Let me tell you something! Someone who dies and rises again, well, that's rather divine, don't you think!?"

"Yeah, yeah, whatever," Mohammad dismissed his incantations, "but it's a historical fact the Council of Nicea was the first time in history an entire church's hierarchy gathered to set doctrine...setting doctrine by mortal men...and if that wasn't enough, it was at the bidding of the Roman Emperor."

"Well, what about you? You never set foot in Jerusalem!"

"Yes, I did!" Mohammad shouted.

"No, you went there in a dream! You only dreamt you went to Jerusalem."

Mohammad's eyes widened in anger.

"So, I'll ask you again. What are you doing at a conference of the gods? You're certainly not a god! And you certainly don't have the patience of a saint!" Jesus gestured at his sheath. "What, the first time something doesn't go your way, you reach for a weapon!"

Mohammad's nostrils flared behind his mask. Instinctively, he felt his hand moving toward his sword.

"Ah, ha, you see!" Jesus shouted.

"God representing Islam is around here somewhere I am certain. You can't miss him. He'll be wearing a mask much like mine. He just wanted me to attend the conference as...well...no matter. It's none of your business. I don't have to explain myself to you."

Jesus glanced around the hotel lobby in a mocking manner, "Oh, does your god carry a scimitar as well?" he smiled, as he turned back toward Mohammad.

Mohammad tried heartily to withhold his emotion but alas he burst into laughter, as he said, "Ah, I have missed our invigorating discussions. They are intoxicating, Jesus," as they gave each other a bear hug. From their embrace Mohammad stepped back, and said, "Oh, I have truly missed our banter."

"Yes, as have I. We must not let so much time go by. We must get together more often," said Jesus.

"So, how have you been my friend?" Mohammad asked.

"Well, up to now, pretty well."

"This mix-up with the reservation has you upset? Don't let these hotels get you down. You can bunk with me."

"Really, you don't mind?"

"Got a room to myself, come on," said Mohammad, as he put his hand on Jesus' shoulder. "Screw these guys. Stay with me."

"Thanks, that's really nice of you, Mohammad, but...uh...your voice. You don't sound like your old self."

"Yeah, I'm coming down with a sore throat."

"You didn't go swimming in the canals, did you?"

"Oh, no! That's illegal but I wouldn't even if it was legal. Over the years I've heard they have been...,"

"Ah, excuse me...uh...Jesus...Nazareth...Christ," said the clerk at the front desk. "If you'll just sign this registration card...just as a formality so we know who is staying at the hotel. Oh, and if you would do so as well, Mr. Mohammad," the clerk said, as he handed each of them a pen.

Mohammad leaned in toward the clerk, and scowled, "Just be sure you don't dare charge me for more than a single room rate just because you guys screwed up and lost my friend's reservation," Mohammad scolded him, as he once again placed a hand on his scabbard.

The clerk nervously shook his head, "No, sir, no sir!"

"You're going to scare someone into a heart attack one of these days, Mohammad."

"Ah," Mohammad grunted dismissively, "I consider it part of my charm."

"I'm telling you people are sensitive to this kind of stuff nowadays. If somebody dies, you've got to answer to my dad for it."

Mohammad simply shook his head.

Jesus turned toward the desk clerk and said, "Oh, by the way, I would like to have my feet washed."

"Oh, you'll find the Pantheon Hotel has a wonderfully wide range of facilities, Mr. Jesus. The rooms are equipped with a wonderful foot washer and massager that stands upon a platform in the shower and you simply slide your foot...,"

"Actually, I was hoping for a woman...uh...to wash my feet. It's...uh...kind of a tradition."

The desk clerk grinned and nodded. "Of course. I understand perfectly, sir," he said, as he looked from side to side and upon seeing no one within earshot reached into his coat pocket, pulled out a business card and handed it to the guest.

"Call Venetian Ecstasy at any time…day or night; they'll accommodate any fetish you might have."

"Well, I was hoping for a woman with long flowing hair—-and oil—-it's important that oil be used."

"Oh, take my word for it, Mr. Jesus, Venetian Ecstasy has a wide assortment of scented oils, and a woman with long flowing hair won't be a problem," he smiled slyly. "If you prefer, I could arrange an appointment for you."

"Oh, yes, that would be wonderful."

"Very well," the clerk nodded.

"Thank you," Jesus smiled gratefully.

"I'll let you know as soon as I've arranged it," said the desk clerk, as he took the now completed registration card, and used the Spanish pronunciation when he asked him, "Is that pronounced, Hay Zeus, by any chance?"

Christ looked up in mild surprise not accustomed to being addressed in that manner.

The clerk did not pursue it, but said, "If you're interested there's a wonderful Tapas restaurant just three blocks from here."

Somewhat taken aback Jesus stammered, "Uh, thank you."

"Here's your key, Mohammad, and here's one for you as well, Mr. Christ. The elevators are to your right, and you're on the sixth floor. Your room number is 6—-6—-," the desk clerk paused for affect, and continued with the final digit 4," and burst into laughter. "Sorry, a bit of hotel humor considering the convention you are with."

Mohammad and Jesus stared unamused at the hotel clerk.

The clerk then felt uneasy, and stuttered, "Uh…uh…enjoy your stay at the…uh…Pantheon Hotel. If there is anything I can do for you, gentlemen, do not hesitate to…,"

"You will not speak to us again," Mohammad told him bluntly.

It was only then the registration clerk saw for the first time the sword dangling in its sheath at Mohammad's side and the clerk's eyes widened in terror.

Mohammad glanced at his sword then focused his line of sight on the clerk. Do not be concerned. I am an expert with a scimitar in my hands. You wouldn't feel a thing."

"Uh...yes...Sir...Mohammad. I apologize, Sir...Mohammad."

"I'm not English. It's simply Mohammad," he chastised the clerk.

"Yes, well, you'll have to check that sword with hotel security as there are no weapons allowed in the hotel," said the clerk, as his hands shook severely in his anxious state of mind.

Mohammad grasped his sword as if wary the desk clerk would attempt to grab it from him, but he relaxed his grip as he realized there was no threat. "Will it be locked in a safe?"

"Absolutely, sir...uh...I mean Mohammad." the clerk nodded.

"All right, I'll allow you to store it for me, but understand something. If it is lost or stolen, it will be you—-not the hotel—-who will answer for it," said Mohammad, behind dark, penetrating eyes.

"I'll bring it to you after I have seen if my room is acceptable," Mohammad said in a harsh tone.

The desk clerk nodded awkwardly and as Mohammad and Jesus walked toward the elevator, he swallowed hard and muttered to himself, "And I've got to work this entire weekend with this group."

Chapter 12

Later, when Bob was speaking with the desk clerk, he saw Ben attempting to get his attention across the lobby and he said, "Excuse me a moment."

"But, we're almost finished here with...,"

"I'll be right back."

As Bob approached Ben, a sound came from the lobby behind them, "Moo."

"Tell me you didn't," said Ben, as he stared sternly at Bob.

"Well...,"

"The cow is revered as a symbol of life, not as a god," Ben explained. "Hinduism would be described more as a way of life than a religion."

"Oh," Bob cringed.

The desk clerk who now noticed what was occurring literally jumped over the counter and ran to the two men on the far side of the lobby. "Sirs, you'll have to get that...that beast removed from the lobby immediately."

Ben nodded and quickly moved into another one of his adlibs as he responded with the affectation of being insulted. "Excuse me? Were you addressing us? That beast to whom you refer is not with us. We merely approached it out of curiosity. He must have wandered into your lobby on his own, I'm sure. Is this the kind of establishment you are running here?"

"But...,"

"Are animals literally free to wander in at any time?"

"Uh...,"

"The sanitary conditions or lack thereof, well, I must say that would be quite appalling."

"Uh...,"

"I trust this is not the manner in which you will be treating your guests during the remainder of our stay in your hotel, or we shall be forced to find other accommodations."

"Oh, sir, I am so sorry. I hope you will understand my angst upon seeing an animal in our lobby."

"Your angst is of no concern to me," Ben replied indifferently.

"Please, please accept my sincerest apology."

"I will only promise to consider it," Ben said with an arrogant affectation, "but may I add that another accusation of this magnitude...,"

"No, sir, I promise it shall never happen again."

"Very well, off with you then and take your new found friend with you before it drops a deposit on your lobby floor and you find yourself with a dozen lawsuits from guests slipping in cow manure."

The clerk swallowed hard, grabbed the rope around the cow's neck and pulled to lead the animal out.

"Uh," uttered Ben, "It might be better to take it out the back way instead of through the front entrance."

"Oh, yes, indeed. Good thought," the clerk replied, as he quickly reversed course.

During this entire exchange Bob had been nodding repeatedly in admiration of Ben's quick thinking, and after the clerk departed he grinned and said, "You have a gift, you know."

"Not **A** gift...I have many gifts."

Bob did not dispute him as his grin widened.

"Better let me have a look at the roster," said Ben, as he grabbed the clipboard. Ben perused it and studied the list of names for several minutes with a skeptical eye. Before he was finished, however, the desk clerk reappeared...his hand raised to his earpiece.

"Now what?" Ben feigned irritation. "Has a lion created a game trail through your lobby?"

"Sir, I am not accusing, merely inquiring...,"

"I understand the distinction. Out with it," Ben deadpanned.

"I have been advised that we are having some difficulty in getting a rather large person through the entrance who is apparently stuck in the lotus position."

"That would be Buddha," Bob interjected. "He's with our group."

That raised an eyebrow of another clerk standing nearby, who remarked, "May I suggest he may enjoy the all you can eat buffet which is presently being served on our Garden Terrace overlooking the Grand Canal."

Ben took a couple of steps toward the clerk, eyed him coldly, and verbally skewered him, "That is wholly inappropriate."

Chapter 13

As Ben and Bob entered Harry's Bar to relax over a drink, Ben scanned the room, and asked, "What's the particular fascination about this place?"

"It's long been frequented by the famous—-Ernest Hemingway, Charlie Chaplin, Orson Welles, Truman Capote, Aristotle Onassis all relaxed and ordered drinks at Harry's Bar," said Bob.

"Hmm, so nobody who's current. Funny how an establishment can lure in the general public because people from the past frequented it, which means we just might be the most famous and illustrious people to visit Harry's Bar in quite some time," Ben noted.

Bob shrugged. "We're not exactly famous."

"My point exactly," Ben smirked, "though we might be famous in a couple of days if all goes well."

"Gentlemen, welcome to Harry's Bar. Two?" asked the host.

Both men nodded.

"This way please," the host led them past a few tables to one against the wall. "Your waiter will be with you shortly. Would you like some water?"

Ben smiled. "No, thanks, we'll be ordering drinks, as I'm sure the water is not free and we would be charged for it."

The host inhaled through his nostrils deeply but held his tongue. "Very well," he nodded and stepped away.

"Good one," Bob nodded in approval. "By the way, besides being frequented by famous dead people, Harry's Bar is known for its very dry martinis and is credited with the invention of the Bellini, a tall cocktail that combines sparkling wine and peach puré, as well as Carpaccio—-a dish...,"

"Yes, I know," Ben interjected, "a dish of raw beef dressed with a mustard sauce but no matter what is served with it, I hardly consider it tasty," Ben differed.

A waiter approached brought them each a bottle of water, and it fell to Ben again to reject the oft pushed liquid. They each proceeded to order a Bellini to get into the spirit of Venice.

When their drinks were served, they raised their glasses in a toast, as Ben said, "Not to get ahead of ourselves or take anything for granted, but to yet another successful endeavor," as they clinked glasses.

"Indeed," said Bob, as they each took a sip of their Bellini's, and their eyes told each other what the other was thinking.

Ben looked around, spotted the waiter and raised his hand, "I'd like a beer here."

"And a bourbon and coke for me," Bob called out.

The waiter was most happy to oblige as the bill increased.

When they were served their new drinks, it was Bob who toasted, "To the greatest ballplayer of all-time."

They clanked glasses as Ben waited but when Bob said nothing further, he responded, "Okay, I'll bite. Who's the greatest ballplayer?"

"Babe Ruth, of course," Bob answered without hesitation. The guy amassed 714 home runs, attained a career batting average of .342, and as a pitcher he won twenty-three games in 1916 with an E.R.A. of 1.75 and the next year he won 24 with a 2.01 E.R.A. Nobody, absolutely nobody, has ever matched that combination of hitting and pitching—-not in one person—-he was so great those feats have never been accomplished since. And don't dare mention Ohtani because he is not part of the comparison until he wins twenty games...twice!"

Never to be outdone, Ben boasted, "Oh yeah, well, Honus Wagner is the most underrated ballplayer of all-time. Hall of Famer not withstanding Honus Wagner has never received his just due," Ben declared.

Bob hesitated unsure of what to say or how to respond and that pretty much ended the discussion regarding Babe Ruth, as Ben said, "We're gonna have to make this quick because the cocktail hour for the gods starts in about thirty minutes."

"The gods drink?" Bob asked.

"Heavily," Ben noted. "They have a lot of stress, and we'll need to be there for the sit-down dinner that follows. Don't worry about covering the agenda for the two days of meetings."

"No? I thought I was supposed to review...,"

"No need but you'll need to be there as a host."

"Yeah, if I blew them off, they might get so pissed they blow a hurricane toward Venice and sink it once and for all."

"Hmm, the gods do have a tendency to get angry and overreact," Ben noted.

"You're gonna be there too, though, right?"

"Not immediately but I'll be there a bit later. There are a few things I need to tend to so everything will be ready for tomorrow."

"Oh, great, I have to attend to the gods by myself while you're off shopping in Venice...and...oh, that reminds me, I need to stop at a store."

"What do you have to get?" Ben asked.

"There's a chain of underwear stores in the states and I learned that there's one here in Venice as well. I packed in a hurry and totally forgot to throw some underwear in the suitcase, so I'll stop by the store to pick up some used underwear."

Not sure that he heard Bob correctly, Ben asked, "You need to get what?"

"It's a used underwear chain. They're all over the U.S. The outlets started up when the economy went south."

"Still...used underwear," Ben stated in astonishment.

"Well, you have to remember that they're a fraction of the cost of new underwear because they're slightly streaked...,"

Ben almost gagged.

"No, no, it's not a problem as they've been thoroughly washed and fully sanitized, so they're ready to wear."

"Ohhh," Ben groaned, as he felt his body beginning to wrench into an uncontrollable spasm.

Chapter 14

When the subordinate returned to the same abandoned building, the mossy ground floor felt damper than it did previously during his first meeting. The entity was seated at the table which was as dusty as it was previously.

As the subordinate approached, he glanced at the empty chair where his timid colleague previously sat and he snickered inside himself that he had moved yet another rung upward on the ladder of leadership. He pulled out a chair and confidently sat down. Though sure of himself, he did not speak as he knew enough to wait until he was directed to do so.

The entity was being served coffee by one of his servants while discussing a matter with one of his guards. The tone of their conversation was secretive and hushed though no notice was given to the servant whatsoever as he refilled the entity's cup.

The subordinate could not discern any words that were spoken, and he was careful not to betray that he was listening by not making any bodily gestures such as leaning or turning an ear toward the conversation. He perceived they were discussing a matter of some importance. The guard acknowledged the end of the conversation with a nod to his superior and backed away until he was stationed against the wall.

With a wave of his hand, the entity authorized his subordinate to speak.

The subordinate proceeded to inform his master of the proceedings in San Marco square and furnished him with the information he had gathered.

The entity listened patiently, and when he was finished, the entity asked, "Is that everything?"

"Yes," the subordinate replied, quite satisfied in a job well done, confident his boss would be pleased.

"And this dinner you mentioned, who will be attending?" the entity asked.

"They will all be there…uh…except for those who were dismissed of course."

"Yes, yes," the entity dismissed his caveat as unnecessary with a wave of his hand, arose and gestured for his subordinate to rise also. With a flick of his boney index figure, he gestured for his subordinate to approach. "What is the reason for this assemblage of the gods?"

"That I have not yet ascertained," he answered, as they strolled around the table.

As they circled the table, the entity cupped his hands behind his back as he walked. It was a habit he developed while contemplating a matter of importance. Presently, he was reviewing in his mind the possible reasons for such a gathering. They circled the table once in silence, and again, as the entity continued to ponder Ben and Bob's objective. The entity returned to his seat, and gestured for his subordinate to return to his chair.

As they sat down the entity raised a hand in a gesture for another to join them.

Out of the shadows came the timid subordinate, while the one who was seated at the table turned and his eyes widened in disbelief as he had assumed that the timid man had already been purged.

Before he knew what was occurring, the guard came up behind the all too confident underling and slipped a rope around his neck and pulled it tightly against the subordinate's windpipe.

The underling gagged as he struggled against the rope, desperately reaching with his hands in the hope of loosening it. While within death's grasp, beneath the table his legs kicked wildly causing the clanking of upending cups and saucers atop it.

But his struggling was futile. With a violent, final pull his hyoid bone snapped as the guard garroted him to death.

The guard, his task completed, placed the rope in his pocket and then backed away to resume his place against the wall.

The entity nonchalantly wiped his mouth with a napkin, and casually commented, "He was much too arrogant, don't you agree?"

The timid subordinate nodded rapidly and repeatedly.

"I detest arrogance," said the entity, as he sneered at the now lifeless body slumped in the chair. Slowly, the entity's facial expression ebbed into a sickly smirk, as he added, "Arrogance is not a good quality for a subordinate to possess."

The timid subordinate shook his head repeatedly as nervous perspiration beaded upon his forehead.

"You will learn the reason for this gathering of the gods...the reason he failed to discover."

The wide-eyed subordinate listened intensely leaving no doubt in the entity's mind that the intimidation method had been successful.

"But remember...," a crooked, bony index finger rose to make a point, "do not let anyone know what information you seek...,"

The subordinate continued nodding his head acknowledging his instructions.

"The key to obtaining what you want, is others being unaware that you desire it."

The subordinate considered his master's sage advice, nodded his acknowledgement of it in silence, then bowed and began to back away to depart for his assignment.

"Wait!" the entity called out, as he arose from his chair.

Startled, the underling froze in his tracks and straightened upright, frightened and shaking that what he had just witnessed would befall to himself.

"I have a better idea," said the entity, as he arose and pondered the details of his next move while he circled his high-backed, plush red velvet chair.

The subordinate said nothing as he stood at attention awaiting new instructions in a change of plans. He hoped his body language wasn't conveying his deep anxiety as he desperately attempted to stand as motionless as he could.

The entity gazed upwards at the ceiling...thinking...a habit of his used from time to time as he worked things out in his mind. Slowly, he lowered his gaze until his eyes made contact with his subordinate's line of sight.

The subordinate swallowed hard at his master's intimidating stare.

When the entity resumed his seat, he gestured with a flick of his wrist toward the corpse at the table. "In his arrogance he was correct about one thing. I cannot trust such an assignment to one who is afraid of his own shadow," he said, as he again eyed his subordinate with an icy, steady stare.

The subordinate swallowed hard while he resisted the urge to flee.

"I shall take over this assignment myself."

The guard retrieved the rope from his pocket and moved silently up behind the timid subordinate.

Chapter 15

At the six o'clock cocktail hour the gods mingled freely amongst one another as Bob thought, *if only all the religions of mankind could get along so well.*

As he approached a couple of gods speaking near the middle of the chic ballroom beneath an elegant chandelier, he listened while he played with a small hors d'oeuvre upon his plate so as not to be noticed eaves dropping.

"Do you believe in god…by that I mean the one god of the desert who is the god of Christians, Jews and Muslims?" Yahweh asked, from behind his iron mask.

"Well, I don't understand what the desert has to do with it," Buddha began. "Perhaps that's some symbolism with which I am unfamiliar, but more to the point, monotheism is a foreign concept to me," he said, as he grabbed the hors d'oeuvre tray so deftly from a passing waiter he didn't break the waiter's stride. Buddha popped several appetizing shrimps into his mouth and continued while munching.

"In my time the world was filled with many gods. And as far as the desert goes, one might as well pray to the god of sand because in some obscure section of the globe no doubt there is a holy deity ever watchful over those eternally sifting, minute desert grains."

With an upturned brow, Yahweh asked with some concern, "Do you not believe in a creator god?"

"Well, we do have a creator god," said Buddha, as he scanned those gathered in the ballroom, "Brahma there," he gestured toward a god on the other side of the room. "He is the most important."

Yahweh glanced to his right without really looking, and asked, "And you?"

"In my faith I am revered as an inspirational leader much in the way John F. Kennedy was an inspiring president if I might draw that parallel by way of explanation.

Yahweh scoffed but it didn't deter Buddha as he continued, "However, since so many people worldwide believe I am a god within the Buddhist faith, I was extended an invitation to the conference. After all, it merely takes one person to believe you to be a god to make it so."

Bob now nodded to the two gods as he moved on. He was pleased that the cocktail hour had gotten off to such a good start, but he heard a passing god mutter to another, "I knew John Kennedy; John Kennedy was and continues to be a friend of mine; and let me tell you, Buddha is no John F. Kennedy," he said, as he then erupted into a chortle of mocking laughter.

Bob turned quickly back toward Yahweh and Buddha relieved to find that neither of them heard the comment.

As Bob moved away, however, he gulped as he saw Mohammad enter the ballroom. Concerned that there could be trouble, Bob hurried toward the entrance, and said, "Mohammad, I thought you checked your sword with the concierge."

"I packed several," he responded, as he surveyed the scene of the gods gathered together.

"Uh, you'll need to check that in the cloak room."

Mohammad frowned, and his eyes betrayed a glint of confusion, as he asked, "What is this paranoia that is so rampant regarding weapons? It is a mere ornament, part of my outfit and not to be crude, but I would feel naked without it."

"Yes, well that would be quite an image...uh...but since there are no images of you that shouldn't' be problem, should it?" Bob commented and continued, "No need for embarrassment...just lose the sword please, and then everyone here will be on equal footing."

Mohammad's posture conveyed to Bob that he was a very proud man and not one who took kindly to someone telling him how to dress but after some considerable thought, he said, "Very well," as he turned and headed for the cloak room.

After Mohammad departed Bob turned, shook his head, and muttered, "Good, God!"

"Yes?" sounded dozens of voices from within the ballroom who were within earshot.

"Sorry...figure of speech," Bob muttered.

Bob then spotted a trio of gods eyeing one another only they weren't talking but staring in an angry, fixed triangular gaze.

"Oh, Je," Bob caught himself just as Christ's ear twitched at the sound of what he thought would be someone taking his name in vain.

"That was close," Jesus smiled.

Bob rushed away toward the three gods, pushed between them and introduced himself. "Zeus, Thor, Jupiter how have you been? You all look well...a bit too intense perhaps...but well. I am one of your hosts. My name is Bob."

"We know who you are. We are gods for Chrissake."

"I heard that," shouted Jesus from across the room with a raised index finger.

All three gods surrounding Bob grunted in reply but none of them turned their line of sight away from the others.

Nervously, Bob glanced from one to the other to the other, and asked, "Have you tried the shrimp? Buddha is absolutely raving about it."

"He would eat a tire if you spread barbeque sauce across it," Zeus noted.

It was Thor who finally turned his gaze away from his long-time rivals, looked at Bob sternly, and replied, "Buddha would rave about sole of shoe if he could chew it."

Zeus laughed heartily and commented, "Yeah, you could barbecue filet of shoe and he'd ramble on about its unique flavor and texture."

Jupiter piped in through his laughter, "He once won a Datsun Bluebird in a drawing and thought he'd be sitting down to a delicious Brazilian dinner of exotic fowl."

As the trio enjoyed another laugh at Buddha's expense, Bob was disgusted that some of the gods spoke of Buddha in such a disrespectful manner, so he moved away and departed the group to mingle with others.

Bob continued to be concerned about so many enormous egos gathered in one place. As he meandered through the ballroom, Bob smiled and nodded to those whom he passed and added a brief greeting.

"Good to see you Apollo."

"It's a Darwinian world, my friend," said Apollo gravely.

"Glad to see you have recovered Neptune. Brahma, enjoy the evening. Fortuna, you made good time from Vegas. I am so glad you arrived in time for cocktails. I trust the gaming went well."

"I've still got it," she smiled, as she mockingly threw a pair of dice.

"Isis, you're looking as lovely as ever and Osiris you're...you're looking quite manly."

"Hmm," Osiris grunted.

"Ah, Roma, we're in your part of the world now."

"The entire world is mine," she replied seriously.

And so, the evening progressed as Bob made a point to greet each and every god in the ballroom so as not to slight or offend any one of them.

By seven o'clock Ben arrived and they all sat down to dinner...all the tables placed together so no one would take offense at the seating.

Ben leaned toward Bob, and asked, "How did it go this evening?"

"So far, so good," he replied. "At least there haven't been any fights as yet."

"Good," Ben nodded.

"Indeed," said Bob, "but I don't know how long we can keep the wrath of the gods on a leash if they blow their stacks with one another. They're all like a volcano seething...ready to erupt. You wouldn't believe how they mock their colleagues."

"Okay, we'll keep our eyes on them. In the meantime, I'm gonna need you first thing in the morning. Do you still arise at dawn?"

"Not since Dawn left me."

Ben looked at Bob with a glance that conveyed he was not in the mood for any jokes.

"I sleep in now, why?"

"Well, get up early and have breakfast. We're leaving for Murano at eight o'clock."

"Are we visiting the glass works?" Bob inquired.

"Yes," Ben replied, hesitated, and seemed a bit unsure of where they were headed in the morning. He wondered, "Or are we visiting the island of Burano where they make lace?"

Bob was about to answer when Ben interjected, "Well, no matter, it's on tomorrow's agenda and the transportation has already been reserved. Perhaps it will be an adventure to see at which island we land," he chuckled.

Chapter 16

In the morning Bob explained, "I chartered a vaporetto or rather many of them."

"What are they?" Ben asked.

"It's a motorized water bus."

"Oh, okay."

"If you really cram, you can get a hundred on one of them."

"How many did you charter?"

"Twenty-five," Bob said timidly.

"What!?" Ben shouted.

"Well, they were reserved before you winnowed down the number of gods."

"Hmm," Ben muttered in annoyance.

"Anyway, we've got transportation for the group. I thought a vaporetto would be best, because it's enclosed in case it rains."

After they boarded the water buses and were pulling away from the dock, Bob commented, "I met someone."

"What?"

"Yeah," Bob smiled.

"When," Ben asked surprised?

"Last night as everyone was heading back to the hotel," Bob said slyly.

Ben smirked, "You dog."

"She's really nice too," Bob added.

A sudden realization struck Ben, "You're not starting something with one of the gods, are you?"

"No, no, no," Bob shook his head. "She's an Italian lady from right here in Venice and we really hit it off. My imagination is running wild too, because you know what it would be like dating someone in the most romantic city on earth?"

Ben noticed the glow in Bob's eyes. "Are you in love again...after only one night?"

Bob shrugged, "I told you, she's very nice."

"They're all nice on the first date," Ben chuckled.

Bob then raised his communicator and spoke to the pilot of the vaporetto. "Captain, pull over at San Michele Island for a few minutes."

"What's in San Michele?" Ben asked.

"It's Venice's cemetery island," Bob pointed.

Ben turned and looked, "Oh, yeah, I see."

"Since Venice is an island community, Napoleon thought it was very unsanitary to bury people in Venice, so in the early nineteenth century, he instructed that a cemetery be created on San Michele."

"Okay, so what's with that?"

"Well, I need to get some flowers for my new lady," Bob grinned.

Ben's eyes conveyed suspicion as his eyebrows upturned, "Tell me there's more than just graves on that tiny isle...that there is a florist."

Chapter 17

Bob held a fresh bouquet of flowers as the vaporetto pulled into the dock at the island of Burano.

"I guess we'll be learning about lace today," Bob smiled, as he noticed the leaning tower, and commented, "Of course, Pisa has the most famous leaning tower, but there's a leaning tower here too."

"What is it, some kind of Italian cultural thing?" Ben asked.

Bob shrugged, "Either that, or Italians don't know how to dig foundations very well." Hmm, come to think of it, Venice is sinking as well."

The gangway lowered as Ben and Bob played the good hosts and led the gods onto the island.

As Vulcanus, the god of fire, walked off the vaporetto, he said, "This is going to be fun. First, we get to watch them make beautiful glass of different colors, and then I can do something I've always wanted to try...glass blowing. I think I shall form a tall, voluptuous woman...a glass sculpture as it were...a tribute to womanhood."

"I could be wrong but I don't think they allow the general public to try their hand at glass making," said Mercury. "That would be dangerous as it's very hot business."

"First of all, we're not the general public and secondly you are aware that I am Vulcanus, aren't you?"

The two gods got in each other's face and looked as though there were about to square off, as Ben interjected, "Uh...sorry for the mix-up Vulcanus, Mercury, but we've docked at Burano and we'll be watching some lace making today."

"Oh, what a yawner," said Vulcanus disgustedly.

"You've got to be kidding!" Mercury chimed in. "We'd be better off watching grass grow."

"Well, there certainly isn't much grass in Venice, but you're welcome to search around Burano to see if you find some," Ben retorted.

As the group disembarked, Bob was at dockside checking off everyone's name and he suddenly blurted out, "Oh, Jesus!"

"What is it? What's wrong?" Ben asked with concern.

"No, I mean Jesus, literally. I thought I checked everybody off the list but he's not here."

"Could he have missed getting back on at the cemetery?" Ben inquired.

"Oh, crap!"

"What?"

"Mohammad is missing as well. Neither of them is aboard."

"Are you sure?" Ben asked.

Disgusted, Bob reboarded the vaporetto, grabbed the communicator, searched for the setting for loudspeaker, and announced, "Jesus, Mohammad, please report to the captain immediately."

The other gods gathered on the dock looked at one another and shrugged unaware of what the problem might be.

Bob disembarked once again, glanced around the immediate vicinity and shook his head, "I don't see them anywhere."

"Maybe they did one of their disappearing acts," Ben suggested, but just then Jesus and Mohammad appeared 'round the corner of a building.

"See I told you," Ben boasted, as he pointed.

Bob shook his head, "No way! I tell you they weren't aboard," Bob asserted, as he approached the pair.

"What happened to both of you?"

"We missed the vaporetto," Jesus explained.

"I knew it!" Bob nodded, as he turned to Ben in a manner that expressed, *I told you so.*

"What's all the commotion?" Jesus asked.

"Well," Bob began, but hesitated, as he looked back out over the miles of the watery lagoon. He turned back to Jesus, and reluctantly asked, "You didn't walk...uh...you didn't carry Mohammad on your back, did you? How did you get here?"

Jesus answered with a sly smile, "We took a water taxi, of course, but what I can't figure is how we arrived before you. Did you stop on the way?" Jesus asked, as he eyed the flowers Bob held.

"Oh, a little side trip, nothing important," said Bob, as he turned to the group of gods, and asked, "Are you ready to see how Burano lace is made?"

Subdued muttering could be heard throughout the group, but Bob continued. "Burano is actually a series of several islands linked by bridges and as you may have noticed it is only a forty minutes ride from Venice just seven kilometers away."

"If you don't stop at the cemetery," one of the gods shouted.

His comment was greeted with laughter from the gods to Bob's embarrassment.

"Yes, it's forty minutes if you don't make any stops," Bob acknowledged good humoredly, and continued. "Burano is a prosperous lace making center, and here the women take great pride in their work and their style of lace which is referred to as *punto in aria* or points in the air," Bob smiled, as he looked out over the gods. "Since we have such a large group, we're going to subdivide into smaller groups so we can visit several lace makers simultaneously."

"Why? Do you have to make another stop on the way back as well?" one of the gods asked.

The chortle of laughter was instantaneous.

After the laughter subsided, Bob said, "No, we won't be stopping on the way back, but dividing into smaller groups will allow each of you to have a birds-eye view of the process...in addition to making the tour less time consuming."

"I'd like to make him a lot less time consuming," Apollo muttered under his breath to one of the gods standing nearby.

"When did lace-making become popular?" asked Minerva, the goddess of arts and crafts.

Apollo turned and looked at her with derision. "There's always one, isn't there?" as he shook his head, and muttered, "Who gives a crap?"

"Well, that's a good question," Bob acknowledged Minerva. "Lace making has occurred for many hundreds of years but it became particularly popular around 1500."

Jesus leaned toward Mars who happened to be standing beside him, and said, "That's 1500 A.D."

Mars, the Roman god of war, always confrontational and looking for a fight, took offense, stared at Jesus as he replied, "What? You think I don't know that? Do you think you're better than me? Is that what you're saying?"

Jesus, with arms outstretched and palms up, said, "Peace be unto you, Mars."

"What, you think you can say anything you want and then pull the peace card? Bull shit, man!" he said, as he inched forward getting in Jesus' face.

Jesus turned slightly offering a cheek to Mars as the Roman god of war clenched a fist.

Bob, seeing what was happening raced to get between them before any punches were thrown.

"Hey, hey, hey, settle down. There's no need to fight over anything."

"I never fight," Jesus replied.

"What? Are you kidding me?" Mars protested. "There have been more wars fought in the name of Jesus than all of us here put together."

"Okay, okay, let's just cool off a bit, shall we? No harm, no foul, so let's calm down," Bob coaxed them.

Jesus offered a hand to Mars.

Ares, the Greek god of war approached, and asked Mars enthusiastically, "Would you like me to smack him for you?"

"Get lost," said Mars spitefully, "I fight my own battles."

"Oh, yeah," said Ares, as he grabbed himself and retorted, "battle this."

In an instant, Mars and Ares were on the ground wrestling and swinging wildly as each attempted to land a punch.

Suddenly, they abruptly stopped as they each sniffed the air.

"I smell smoke," said Mars.

"I do as well," Ares agreed.

As they looked up, they saw flames in the distance as fully a quarter of the island was ablaze.

While sitting atop the leaning tower of the San Martino Church admiring the arson's handiwork, Agni, Chu Jung, Gabija, Gerra, Gibil and many others gawked at the blaze along with more than two dozen other gods of fire...all of them staring with great interest, mesmerized by the raging inferno.

The sirens of nearly a dozen fire boats sounded as they raced toward the flaming firestorm.

Chapter 18

The entity approached the lifeless body of his subordinate, the guard standing over him tucking the lethal knotted cord back into his pocket once again. The entity nodded approvingly as he looked toward his guard.

"You are very efficient."

"Thank you, sire."

"As you have seen, I now have two openings on my staff."

"Yes, sire."

"A staff position pays considerably more than the wages of a guard. Would you be interested in making more money...in a promotion from guard to a member of my staff?"

The guard held up his hand, palm facing his master and said, "No, no, thank you, sire. I appreciate the offer, but no I'm good in my present employ."

The entity appeared genuinely mystified as to why his guard would refuse such a promotion, but he shook his head and did not pursue the matter any further.

"Take him away and dispose of the lad."

"Yes, sire," said the guard as he bent over to grab the deceased.

"Let him be greeted into eternity with the flames of the furnace."

"Yes, sire," the guard acknowledged his orders as he dragged the body from the room while closing the door behind him.

Now alone in the ground floor of the abandoned mansion, the entity approached a wall mirror and saw his own bony index finger rise to make another point, as he commented to his mirrored image. "The most crucial aspect of surprise is not revealing you are there."

Chapter 19

Ben said, "I banned all of the gods of fire for their complacency in watching the blaze."

"How did they take being banned?"

Ben thought for a moment as the question took him a bit by surprise. "You know, I think upon witnessing the fire they would say that it was worth it."

"Hmm, yes, they do enjoy their fires, don't they?"

"In any event," Ben continued, "the size of our gathering has dwindled by another couple dozen, and in considering the fire we're going to have our hands full sooner than I had foreseen."

"Are you saying the fire was set deliberately?" Bob asked.

"Oh, no question about it," Ben confirmed. "Luckily, the fire boats were on the scene quickly and got the blaze under control and prevented it from spreading."

"Were any of the Burano residents injured?"

"Some were treated for smoke inhalation but they'll be okay and no one was killed."

"Well, that's a relief. Did they save the lace shops?"

Ben shook his head, "Some of them were completely destroyed. A lot of lace was destroyed."

"I imagine lace ignites rather quickly," Bob commented with dejection.

"You liked that lace, did you?"

Bob nodded, "Yeah, it's pretty intricate."

"Well, don't be too depressed because the ladies that make it aren't. Oh, they're disappointed but I heard a number of them commenting that orders will simply be delayed and another laughed that they'll have good job security for quite some time now."

"Amazing how resilient people can be sometimes despite what they've lost."

"Indeed," Ben agreed.

"Do the authorities have any idea how it started?"

"They've determined that it was definitely arson," Ben answered without hesitation.

"Did they catch who set it?"

"No, and at this point in their investigation they don't have any idea who started it, but I do," said Ben.

"Who?"

"I'm not ready to say just yet."

Bob didn't take offense, as he knew Ben would tell him when he was absolutely sure and at the appropriate time.

"So, where are we heading next?" Bob asked.

"We continue our tour as if nothing out of the ordinary has happened. They all know about the fire now, of course, but we won't say anything about it being arson. We stop on the island of Murano for a short tour of the glass factories and then we return to Venice."

Bob nodded in confirmation.

After they disembarked the vaporetto on the island of Murano, Bob presented a bit of history, as he escorted the group.

"All of the glass production was moved off the mainland in 1291 to this island of Murano."

"Why?" asked one of the gods.

"To avoid a fire hazard in Venice," Bob answered.

"Like the one we just saw on Burano?" Apollo asked ironically.

"Apollo, can you please bottle the sarcasm?" Bob asked with impatience.

Apollo responded with an obtuse gesture but didn't comment further.

Many of the gods nodded in agreement with Bob as they were becoming quite fed up with Apollo as well, while another of the gods asked, "With so much glass production centralized in such a relatively small area, didn't that simply transfer the fire hazard from Venice to Murano?"

"That is absolutely true," Bob answered. "Venice was a great power both on the sea and economically from about twelfth century on, and the rulers didn't want anything to interfere with that power, so they moved the glass production to Murano. Of course, the power of Venice plunged dramatically five hundred years later, not by fire, but with the discovery of America."

"Yeah, that makes sense," said one of the gods to another, "the trade routes from Spain, Portugal, France, the Netherlands and England to name a few would not have backtracked to Venice."

Bob nodded in agreement, "Correct."

Once again Ben and Bob broke the gods into several smaller groups to visit several glass makers simultaneously.

Chapter 20

Once back at the Pantheon Hotel seated in the sauna Ben and Bob mingled with the gods. It was part of Ben's plan formulated many months ago.

"You know, there's something I don't understand," Bob said quietly.

"I'm sure it's more than one thing, but what is it?" Ben asked.

"If our assignments originate from a higher power, is he here?"

"Is who here?"

"The higher power," Bob clarified, "the one who passes out the assignments that we endeavor to solve."

"Oh, I work through an intermediary. I never speak directly to the Man," Ben explained.

"Oh, okay," Bob nodded, unsure whether Ben was joking, as Bob glanced through the steam at several gods who had joined them.

"Well, are you ready to go?" Ben asked.

"I'm certainly sweated out."

"Okay, we'll hit the shower and head to dinner."

"No objection from me," said Bob, "I'm famished."

After they showered and dressed, Ben said, "That was certainly refreshing."

"Yeah," Bob agreed.

At the restaurant the maitre'd escorted the duo to their table and they caught a partial conversation between a pair of gods, as Terminus commented on the pasta.

"Mmm, this is really good."

"Of course, you'd like Italian food," said Hypnos sarcastically, "you're a Roman god."

Between bites Terminus asked, "What is Hypnos anyway? What are you a god of?"

"I'm the god of sleep. Hypnos...get it?"

"Ah," Terminus acknowledged nodding.

"And you, Terminus?"

"I'm the guardian of boundaries…Terminus. Get it?" he asked, in a gotcha moment.

As Bob sat down opposite Ben, he shook his head, and commented, "I just can't believe how often the gods nearly come to blows."

"Yeah, they do have their arguments, don't they," Ben agreed.

"I'm truly stunned by it. It's like they all have a hair trigger," said Bob, as he picked up his menu to peruse it. "I'll tell you one thing though. I've got to really start watching what I say," as he lowered his voice, and continued. "I'm in this habit of saying Jesus or God so often…I mean, I wasn't aware of my language until this weekend."

Ben nodded as he perused the menu.

"So, what do you have a taste for tonight?" Bob asked.

"Oh, I'm going Italian all the way," said Ben.

"Absolutely," Bob concurred, "Italian it is."

Dionysus, the Greek god of wine had obviously imbibed too much of his favorite red and wobbled toward one of the tables.

"Hey, Jeeeeesus, my man," he slurred his speech. "How the hells are you?"

Uncomfortable, at the intrusion, Jesus merely nodded hello and resumed his meal without speaking.

Dionysus steadied himself by placing his hands on the table, but he put too much of his weight on the table as he leaned on it. The opposite side of the table jerked upward as dishes rattled and several glasses of water sloshed their contents onto the tablecloth. Mohammad grabbed his glass before its contents spilled completely though some water splashed onto his hands.

"Hey, Jesus! Did you see that? I just laid hands on the table. Get it? Hey, check that water it might be wine now," Dionysus laughed heartily.

Jesus was not amused.

"Hey, Jesus, did you walk on water to cross the Grand Canal?"

"I took the Rialto Bridge across," Jesus replied without humor.

"So, when you say a prayer, do you just talk to yourself?" he laughed, "Dear Me," as Dionysus continued chuckling, then tapped on Mohammad's mask, "Hello? Is anybody home?"

"Look, pal, we don't want any trouble," said Mohammad, as he arose and pulled back a portion of his garment exposing his sword.

"Dammit Mohammad," Bob shouted, arising from his chair. "Will you once and for all lose the damn sword!?"

Dionysus shook his hands in mock terror. "Oh, you've got a sword. I'm really scared. I suppose you wore that to the sauna today so you could perform some circumcisions."

Yahweh, at an adjacent table, took offense at that and arose flashing a look of contempt mingled with disgust, as Mohammad went chest to chest with Dionysus.

Mohammad's eyes flamed in anger, as Bob stepped in between them.

"Dionysus, didn't we say that gods of all vegetation were excused?" Bob asked.

"I'm the god of wine," he hiccupped. "I am not before nor am I during the grape. There is a difference. I am after the grape has been harvested."

"Well, at the very least I think you should call it a night, Dionysus. Come along," said Bob, as he glanced back at Mohammad and bid him to relax. "Please sit and try to enjoy your dinner."

"Humph," Mohammad grunted, as he took his seat.

"On second thought," he flipped his napkin onto his plate disgusted, "I've lost my appetite. What do you say we get out of here?"

"Well, there's a concert tonight in Piazza San Marco that might be fun and rather relaxing to attend," said Jesus.

"Yeah, fine," Mohammad snapped, "as long as it's out of here. Come on, let's go."

Chapter 21

The Grand Canal shimmered under the glow of a full moon as gondoliers glided slowly past the orchestral strains of a piece performed from Vivaldi's best-known work, The Four Seasons. Appropriately, Antonio Vivaldi was a Venetian composer, born and raised in Venice. The concert conducted in Piazza San Marco was free to anyone who strolled by and cared to listen.

Mohammad, hidden as ever behind his iron mask, walked with Jesus past the bell tower. The brick campanile is majestically capped by a pyramid spire with a golden archangel, Gabriel, sitting atop it...a weathervane that turns with the winds.

When an evening breeze arose from the lagoon, the weathervane turned as it usually did only this time the archangel, Gabriel came alive as he raised his gaze skyward.

A black-feathered, winged creature flew above Venice and as it drew closer, Gabriel saw its yellowish, evil eyes above a sharp, jagged beak. As the creature circled and scanned the scene below, it floated upon the air currents with its enormous wing span. As it descended it revealed its razor-sharp talons.

A woman's shriek alerted Jesus. Jesus turned abruptly in the direction of the shrill sound and saw a woman pointing skyward. Jesus looked up to see the approaching menace. Silently, Mohammad stepped away creating separation between himself and Jesus.

The winged-creature swooped past Gabriel and descended rapidly toward Jesus who now noticed his friend Mohammad was many paces away from him. Gabriel saw that Jesus was vulnerable and leapt from the tower.

"Kill him," an angry voice growled from behind an iron mask.

In an instant Gabriel knocked Jesus to the ground pushing him out of harm's way while simultaneously grabbing and swinging his sharp silver blade. But his effort was futile. He swung his blade at empty air missing the creature.

Jesus arose startled and wide-eyed in disbelief at the sudden attack.

Ben and Bob came rushing toward him, as Ben yelled, "Hit the deck!"

Jesus spun around and fell to the ground as the dark creature swiped at him with its sharp talons. The creature missed its mark while the iron-masked Mohammad sped from the square into the Doge's palace.

Ben continued his pursuit of the iron-masked villain as he signaled for Bob to circle around the other way.

Jesus picked himself up and quickly ducked into a shop on the perimeter of St. Mark's Square where he grabbed a bow and arrow.

As he exited the shop, Jesus muttered, "Turn the other cheek, my ass! Not to a creature of the night I won't," as he shot at the flying creature arrow after arrow into the night in rapid succession. Jesus, however, was not a marksman with such a weapon. Two arrows bounced off the brick bell tower, three others missed the creature and whistled into the darkness, while another hit the bell...the clang of the echo resounding throughout the Piazza.

For this assignment, Ben and Bob had studied the floor plans of every building in Venice and they knew the Doge's palace inside and out. The duo struck at the precise moment when the perpetrator was exactly where they wanted him. Wherever he might flee, they wouldn't lose him.

As Ben entered the front of the palace, Bob picked a lock and slipped in the back.

Outside the palace Jesus was out of arrows. He dropped the bow, moved quickly to the water's edge and grabbed at a gondolier's beechwood oar. He strained and grunted until he had freed it from its fórcola.

As Jesus moved back into the Piazza, the creature swooped again.

Jesus swung the twelve-foot oar and caught the dragon-like monster flush across the side of its head.

In a shrieking death-screech the creature crashed to the ground slamming against the cement and splattered.

"Ah, ha!" Jesus yelled, "right across the temple! How's that for irony? Only you're not going to rise on the third day!"

Jesus took a deep breath, his heart beating rapidly from the rush of adrenalin. Slowly, his heart rate slowed and his breathing returned to normal.

Jesus began to relax as he felt the danger had passed when the winged-lion of Venice suddenly jumped from its perch atop the marble pillar and leapt to the ground at the feet of Jesus.

Startled, Jesus stood perfectly still as he looked into the eyes of the lion. The lion flapped its wings while it scratched its claws against the cement. Jesus thought the lion was about to pounce as it leaned back on its haunches poised to strike, but unbeknownst to Jesus, a creature was rising from the lagoon behind him. As it came to surface, it pulled itself out of the lagoon and slithered toward Piazza San Marco. It was the same creature Ben had fought when he and Bob arrived in Venice.

The winged-lion leapt.

Instinctively, Jesus ducked.

The lion soared over Jesus, opened its mouth and snared the creature. As the guardian of Venice, the winged-lion clamped down with its powerful jaws and sharp incisors upon the creature's neck. The monster shrieked in agony. The winged-lion spun like a shot-put thrower and heaved the creature back into the lagoon, bloodied and wailing near death as it splashed into the water. The winged-lion turned back toward Jesus, nestled down on the ground and bowed its head.

Jesus smiled, "Well, it's nice to know I have a friend like you," as he gently patted the lion's head.

Chapter 22

Inside the Doge's palace Ben raced past the display cases housing old weapons from the sixteenth century. Suddenly he stopped, as he had a thought. He turned toward one of the displays and smashed the glass with his booted foot. He reached in and grabbed a long silver single-hand thrusting blade known as a rapier. He swashed in the air a couple of times to get the feel of it and then continued his pursuit.

Ben saw the masked figure in the distance as he raced across the Bridge of Sighs...the famous enclosed white limestone bridge that spans the canal which divides the Doge's palace from the prison. With stone bar windows, it was the last view of magnificent Venice that prisoners saw as they were taken to their cells...thus they sighed.

The iron masked villain saw Bob racing toward him from the rear of the prison. He was not worried in the least that a mere mortal could stop him, but Bob reached into his pocket and pulled out a small metallic object.

The entity eyed him and stared at the mysterious object as Bob faced him while Ben closed in on him from the opposite direction.

The entity growled and then raced toward Bob.

Suddenly and violently the entity slammed against an invisible force field. He was knocked backwards and to the ground by the powerful obstruction.

Groggy, he picked himself up and retreated as Ben pulled an identical metallic object from his pocket, raised it and once again the force field abruptly stopped the fleeing entity knocking him down again.

He again picked himself up and the only route left to him was to duck into the first cell on the left across the Bridge of Sighs. He wasn't worried in the least about being trapped because neither bars nor walls would hold him for long.

As he entered the small cell, Bob was close behind him. The metallic object was equipped with a keyboard and Bob punched in several numbers as Ben entered and input several numbers into his device as well.

The force field completely enveloped the iron-masked entity and formed four invisible walls. The entity was suspended in midair...his feet dangled above the floor of the cell as the invisible barrier completely encompassed him and prevented him from leaping up and away. He was trapped, completely contained.

"The DNA specific repellent force field system you developed has worked to perfection," Ben said, genuinely pleased.

Bob nodded, "Thanks," as he smiled proudly.

Of course, since the force field was not calibrated to either their DNA, Ben was free to reach through the force field and remove the iron mask. Ben did so unceremoniously and revealed his identity.

"So, Phosphoros, we meet at last," Ben smirked.

Bob looked on quizzically unfamiliar with the name.

Ben made the introductions. "Bob, allow me to introduce you to the Greek god of the morning star, Phosphoros, otherwise known in the Roman culture as Lucifer. The two names are interchangeable."

Bob's mouth dropped open...agape with surprise.

Phosphoros snarled.

"You out smarted yourself, Phosphoros. I knew you weren't Mohammad. He would never have commanded anyone to kill Jesus as you attempted in the square."

The monster-like creature glared at Ben through hateful eyes.

"Besides, Mohammad didn't receive an invitation to the conference, because he is not a god," Ben smirked again, "he is in fact a prophet. Your explanation for attending was seen exactly as what it was...a ruse."

Lucifer continued to stare through a veil of hateful rage, as he possessed an unbounded loathing for his captors as he struggled to free himself to no avail.

Ben's smirk evolved into a grin, as he said confidently, "No one knew the reason for assembling the gods in Venice, not even Bob knew the specifics of our assignment. I knew that upon hearing of such a conference, you could not resist the temptation to appear. You see, temptation is your weakness, Phosphoros, and all of those like you—-temptation—-it overwhelms you and you cannot help yourself."

The entity continued to eye Ben with loathing while struggling and straining against the force field in a futile effort to free himself.

"You see, you are the purpose of the conference, Lucifer," as Ben used both names interchangeably. "You are the reason we assembled the gods, and the purpose of the conference has now culminated in absolute triumph."

Suddenly, Phosphoros vanished.

Bob was startled by Lucifer's sudden disappearance and somewhat bewildered he looked at the device he held in his hand thinking it had failed.

Ben raised his hand in a gesture for Bob not to be concerned, "Don't worry."

Ben then turned his gaze to the specific area within the cell where they last saw Lucifer. "Yes, you can make yourself undetectable, Phosphoros, but as you are now undoubtedly aware that does not mean freedom of movement. Make yourself invisible and you still cannot pass through closed doorways, or through walls; you cannot move from one place to another; cannot free yourself from the force field in which you are presently imprisoned. Whether visible or invisible, here in this cell in Venice, whether the door is locked or unlocked, whether the door is wide open or completely removed, you are trapped for all time—-encompassed in the DNA specific force field. Think of all those who come to Venice, who visit the Doge's Palace, who cross the Bridge of Sighs, and view the first cell on the left. Perhaps you will show yourself to some of those who pass by but whether you elect to show yourself or not, Lucifer, you are trapped within this cell...frozen in place for all time," said Ben, as he gestured to Bob with a tilt of his head that it was time to leave.

Momentarily, Phosphoros made himself visible, the countenance of his ugly anger evident, as he snarled for a few seconds and then went invisible again.

Ben and Bob departed the cell, walked back onto the Bridge of Sighs and paused to catch their breath in a brief but well-deserved respite.

Ben smiled at their achievement of a job well done, and commented, "From this point forward, with him trapped in that cell, mankind cannot blame Lucifer for the evil men do."

Bob nodded in agreement, "Yeah, he will literally be locked away for all time because the DNA specific force field is self-perpetuating. It generates its own power and maintains its own power supply from the force field itself. No batteries need be included," Bob smiled in admiration of his handiwork.

The End

Epilogue

After completing their assignment, Ben and Bob lingered on the Bridge of Sighs to catch their breath, as Bob asked, "So, how did it all go down?"

"Well, before the conference gathered in Piazza San Marco, I was able to contact Jesus. I knew he and Mohammad have a great respect for one another but I cautioned Jesus that Mohammad had not been invited since he wasn't a god. Nevertheless, I informed Jesus that someone had appeared as Mohammad...an imposter...but I asked Jesus to play along so as not to tip him off.

Bob nodded his acknowledgement, "Well done, especially since we didn't know who the imposter was at that point."

"You were right about them not being on board the water taxi. Phosphoros, or Lucifer as we know him, and Jesus did cross the lagoon on a water taxi but they split up as soon as they docked in Burano. In fact, when we saw them rounding the corner on Burano, they had just met up."

"It was Phosphoros who set the fire?"

"Oh, yeah, and all the while the other gods thought it was Mohammad behind the iron mask."

Bob nodded, "There are no images of Mohammad," Bob pointed out.

"Correct and Phosphoros used that to his advantage. It would be understandable for all the gods assembled that he wouldn't want his image seen."

"It was somewhat ingenious actually, and you're right. No one would question him wearing that iron mask. It never ceases to amaze me how deception is so easily believed," Bob commented, as he shook his head.

"Precisely," said Ben, "but like I told him; he outsmarted himself. He thought he could get away with impersonating Mohammad.

Phosphoros deceived himself although Jesus unknowingly almost blew our whole assignment."

"How so?"

"It was when Jesus was speaking to Mohammad's imposter and saying he shouldn't be in Venice because it was for gods only...no prophets allowed at the conference. If the gods had picked up on that, they might have booted him out and we'd have lost our chance to imprison him," Ben noted.

Bob nodded his agreement. "Oh, yeah, we got lucky there."

"Indeed, we did," Ben agreed whole-heartedly.

"Something I don't understand though. Why did Phosphoros set a fire on Burano?" For what purpose?"

Ben shrugged, "Because that's what Phosphoros does...sets fires...wreaks havoc," Ben offered. "I was worried though before we entered the codes arming the DNA repulsion unit."

Bob was taken aback by that. He had already informed Ben that he designed the apparatus exactly per Ben's specifications, and he wondered, "Why?"

"What do you mean, why? I kept thinking about the parking garage—-all those trunks you opened unintentionally."

Bob chuckled, "Oh, not to worry, I'll perfect that one day too," he said.

A refreshing breeze kicked up from the lagoon, and Bob looked out at Venice from the Bridge of Sighs. As he gazed toward the Venetian lagoon in the distance, Bob inhaled the sea air, and sighed."

"Ah," Ben chuckled, "you sighed."

"Oh, that I did," Bob laughed, "on the Bridge of Sighs. Gosh, it sure is a beautiful city, isn't it?"

"Don't get too comfortable," said Ben. "We might get another job assignment at any moment."

"Yeah, they do come fast and furiously, don't they?"

"Yeah, there's a lot of evil out there for us to combat."

"Hmm," Bob nodded his agreement.

"Well, what do you say? Shall we head back to the Pantheon Hotel and get packed," Ben suggested.

"Yeah, and how about I buy us one last drink before we depart Venice."

"It's a deal," Ben agreed.

Postscript

As Ben and Bob strolled across the lobby of the Pantheon Hotel they heard the melodic strains of Vivaldi's Allegro Pastorale. When they took a seat at the hotel bar, they ordered their drinks, and Bob said, "Vivaldi was born in Venice, you know. Sad though."

"Oh? How so?" Ben asked.

"He traveled to Vienna which is pretty much where all the great musicians headed, but he died in poverty just two years after his arrival and was buried in a mass grave. It wasn't until after his death that his music was truly appreciated."

"That is sad that he never experienced an appreciation for his music," Ben agreed, as the bartender delivered their drinks.

Ben and Bob clinked their glasses to toast a job well done.

Unbeknownst to Ben and Bob, the desk clerk spotted them as they entered the lobby and quickly approached them in the bar, and he was obviously in another heated panic.

"Gentlemen, Gentlemen," he beckoned, nearly beside himself in anxiety.

"Now what?" Bob wondered aloud impatiently.

"The Grand Canal is full of barges with a cargo that each captain swears is to be delivered to you here at the Pantheon Hotel."

"Oh? What cargo is that?" Ben inquired.

"It is a shipment of 1,250 golf carts!" he uttered frantically.

While Ben did a slow turn toward his partner, Bob's eyes widened in surprise as the recollection registered in his mind. He'd forgotten all about the golf carts he ordered.

"They are being delivered to your attention," said the desk clerk. "We have no place to put them and the captains are adamant they are to be unloaded at once."

The desk clerk nervously glanced toward the front entrance where he saw several of the barge captains entering the hotel lobby. "Oh, dear," he exclaimed, and off he went in a hurry in the hope of stopping them before they unloaded the golf carts.

Ben eyed Bob with distinct displeasure but Ben's mind moved rapidly in thought as he quickly deliberated upon the situation.

Bob leaned in toward Ben, and whispered, "Uh…perhaps we should pack more quickly than we thought."

"I'm thinking we shouldn't pack at all," Ben commented, and with a tilt of his head toward the rear of the lobby, he added, "Come on, let's get out of here…out the back by way of the Armory and grab a water taxi from there to the mainland."

While the desk clerk spoke to the captains at the front entrance his back was turned as Ben and Bob slinked away toward the rear exit.

"1,250 golf cars…this is bad, isn't it?" Bob asked rhetorically.

"Well, certainly no one is going to sign off on those golf carts and take possession."

"No," Bob shook his head…his dejection quite visible.

"But the bad part's when you call Jack to explain what happened to his golf carts and why no one took delivery…let alone why the bill isn't paid. Plus, he'll be out the shipping charges to Venice and then the cost of returning them to his shop in North Carolina."

Bob's shoulders slumped as he sighed, "Crap."

"Yep, that's a conversation I'd really like to hear," said Ben with an impish sparkle in his eyes.

Bob shook his head…disheartened that Jack would be so disappointed.

"Yeah, a family business, I'm sure Jack was ecstatic at the sale of 1,250 golf carts in one shot," Ben rubbed it in.

Bob glared at Ben, "You really enjoy it when I get in a jam, don't you?"

"Ah, don't worry about it. Jack knows you…what you're like…so he'll understand."

Bob's eyebrows furrowed in confusion as to what Ben meant by that.

Finally, Ben thought that was enough, and said, "Ah, don't worry about it. We'll be paid handsomely for this assignment and we'll make good on the bill and the transportation costs of shipping them back. Jack will make out quite well...he'll be paid for all of them and then get them back in his inventory and be able to sell them again as used carts just as good as new."

An initial quick nod by Bob gave way to a slightly confused look as Ben's countenance ebbed into a grin.

"What? Why are you grinning?"

"Oh, I was just thinking. When we get back to our rental car, maybe you'll get lucky on our trip back to Rome. I mean since we haven't time to pack...maybe you'll find one of those used underwear outlets along the way."

Other Ben & Bob Adventures

Death in Sedona
Prisoners of Paris
Beware Sundown
In the Land of Eternal Spring
Nostradamus: The First Prophecy
Ghost Shack
Piazza Navona
Purple Mountain Majesties
Discovery
Windy City Terror

About the Publisher

www.ingramcontent.com/pod-product-compliance
Lightning Source LLC
Chambersburg PA
CBHW020605160726
47991CB00002B/875